Paranormal Teacher

Cinna Solomon

Contents

Chapter 1: Meeting Mr.Night

Okay no matter how much you try to spin it, school sucks. I mean angry teachers, bitchy blondes, player jocks, for the above average loser school is a living hell. I hate it. I'm pretty much the biggest loser in school. I have two friends, that's it. One is my emo crazy bitch (in a good way) of a best friend Jane. And the other is my caring sweet Noah. But he's gay, so no romance there.

Jane's got this bleach blonde/ silver hair with black and blue streaks in it. Her brown eyes have a ring of black around them 24/7. Her clothes consist of mostly black and neon clothes. She was your average emo girl. Well scene I guess...? I don't know she tried to explain it to me but I didn't quite get it.... Noah is 6'1 brown hair gray eyes if he wasn't gay I'd be into him. But sadly he is therefore does not swing my way... too bad huh? But both were fairly attractive, were as I was too short standing at 5'1 long wavy black hair. Grossly pale like borderline ghost, not that pretty pale but creepy pale skin. And pale blue eyes. I wore glasses religiously. I mean sure I really didn't need them, they were for show. But the glasses covered my face so I didn't really care. I was deathly thin, no matter how much I ate I was still sickly small. My clothes were mostly jeans and over sized t-shirt with either my black boots or converse. I wasn't exactly fashion conscious, it didn't make sense to me. I watched as all those girls spending hundreds and hundreds of dollars on a pair of jeans or a t-shirt that wouldn't last more than a year, maybe less. Especially in my school, girls and boys in my school change their look and clothes so quick I don't even have time to blink.

My face was always in a book I rarely talked in class or to anyone in general. Teachers stopped calling on me which was just how I liked it. You'd think I'd be a nerd smart but I'm not. I'm pretty average. I'm even failing biology. It's hard okay?? Especially if you have a teacher that sits there gives you a pack of notes tells you to fill them out then talks about her love life. And trust me hearing about a 50 year olds sex life is pretty disturbing.

I walked down the hall way to my locker. I was almost there until I heard someone say "Hayley Lake. Shouldn't you have and gone and killed yourself by now? No one likes you around here. You have like, what two friends? Both being huge losers just like yourself. You're so ugly it should be illegal and you aren't even smart so how do you stay alive. If I were you I would have killed myself by now." I stopped walking and shuddered as I remembered. I've heard those words before. But it's been so long since I've remembered. His pitch black eyes filled with no sympathy no remorse, nothing but rage and hate. I was lost in my thoughts when I heard a voice say "Blake you're completely fake. I mean your boobs aren't even real anymore. And your nose, how much did daddy have to pay for that?" Jane said coming up from behind me with Noah right on her tail.

The dumb blonde looked at Jane and Noah and said "All this coming from the emo bitch and gay wimp. Pl-lease. Like you two are really scary." Jane looked at her and said "well if you don't think I'm scary now just wait till you'll have to get another nose job." Blake stiffens and walked away.

I smile and hugged Jane. "Thanks!" I said.

"No problem, anything for you. And making the queen bitch mad is just a bonus."

"But you know. Blake's gotta point Hun. You are beautiful without the glasses. With a bit of work a facial or two and a good tan you'd look ah-mazing." Noah said.

"And some new clothes" Jane piped in.

I smiled at them. "Maybe someday."

"How bout this week?" Noah asked.

"No"

"Next week?"

"No"

"Next month?"

"No"

"Tomorrow?"

"Defiantly not"

"Then when?"

I smiled sweetly "never" I said, and then walked away as the bell ringed. I kept walking as I heard Noah and Jane scream that it'd be a good thing. They said that I'd thank them when they kidnap me and give me a makeover. I laughed to myself. They honestly made my day. The first four periods went my quickly. Being a junior sucked because everything ended up being a hell of a lot harder than last year I made my way to my locker Noah and Jane already waiting for me there.

"So guess what?" Jane asked excitedly. She almost looked like a over happy chipmunk.

"What?" I asked smiling.

"We have a new science teacher!" Noah said.

"Hey I wanted to tell her!" Jane complained.

I smiled "okay so?" besides getting rid of Mrs. Rain I didn't really care about a new science teacher.

"He's soooo hot!" Jane said.

"He's almost editable." Noah added.

"Really?" I asked faking excitement.

"YES!" Jane squealed.

"He's got this black hair and amazing bright blue eyes. He's god damned tall, 6'5 at least. He's a giant compared to me! I wonder if he swings my way...." Noah said drifting off into his own little perverted thoughts.

"I sure hope not!" Jane said.

I just laughed. They were ridiculous. He probably had a cute wife waiting for him at home. "Well I don't believe he's honestly at hot as you say. Let's go. I gotta see his guy."

They laughed at me and we walked to science. We sat in the back, the class room had about 10 huge black lab tables sitting three people each. I stared out the window as Jane and Noah was still fighting about who would get the new teacher. I still thought they were insane. I stopped paying attention as I started to drift off into sleep.

DREAM

I looked around me. I was in the middle of an empty field. I looked around me trees everywhere all but one side, there was a beautiful pool of water with a waterfall running down into it. I went to the water looked down there were little tiny pretty fish. The water was so clear it was breath taking. I know where I am. I was in the woods near my grandmother's house. The last time I was there I was eight. My mother had just died and my dad took me to visit her. I wondered off the little swing grandpa had made for my mom and I found myself here, just where I was standing now. Weird. I looked at my reflection I was eight again. I looked pretty for a child. I wonder what happened between now and then. But I didn't really need to wonder. I knew what happened. I was sitting at the edge of the pool my feet dangling into the water when I heard a growl. I turned around and saw a wolf. It was huge almost the size of a bear. I started to panic. It crept closer my breathing speed up. But as I looked into it eyes I felt calm. I felt save. "Hello." I said.

It just looked at me with eyes that seemed to smile at me. "How are you?" I asked. It still just stared at me. It came up to me and rubbed it head against my tiny body. I laughed as it started to lick my face with its huge tongue.

It suddenly stopped licking me and said "Hayley." I looked at it dumbfounded. It knew my name? "Miss. Lake, please wake up. I do not appreciate you sleeping in my class room. "

Huh? I thought. Then I felt some violently shaking me. The wolf and the lake disappearing from my sight at I found myself staring at the most beautiful pair of blue eye I have ever seen. "You're not a wolf." I said.

END DREAM

Did I really just say that? I thought, mentally slapping myself in the face.

"Yes you did Miss. Lake."

Crap did I just say that too?

"Yes you did. Anyways please do not fall asleep again. Pay attention." I blushed and looked down. Trying to ignore the laughter I heard around me and little remarks about me being such a freak. Noah and Jane looked at me with sympathy in their eyes. I smiled at them reassuringly then turned my attention to the teacher. HOLY SHIT! He really was hot. And crap I just got on his bad side. Yippy....

"Okay now that I have everyone attention," the teacher said looking straight at me. I blushed redder. His face got a little softer and he smiled. "I'm Mr. Night. Yes that's my real last name. I was born with it. Since it's my first day I just want to take the time to get to know you. And answer your questions about me."

I wasn't shocked with Amy raised her hand. Amy was a slut. "Yes Miss..."

"Amy." She said sweetly. He smiled and said "Yes Amy what's your question."

"Are you single?"

He smiled thoughtfully. He looked straight at me for a minute smiled at me with some unreadable expression and said "Yes I am. But I have someone I love very much."

"Oh..." Amy said dejected.

Noah raised his hand next. "How long have you two been going out?"

"Shut up fag." Lisa said quietly so only Noah and I could hear.

Noah blushed and shrunk in his seat. I was pissed as hell. Mr. Night was about to say something when I stood up went up to Lisa and slapped her across the face. It was so quiet you could hear a needle drop. Lisa started to cry as she ran up to Mr. Night hugging him crying her eyes out. "Why did she do that? I was just sitting there and she came up and slapped me. That was so mean! You know, Hayley's always been jealous of me I'm beautiful and guys like me while she's so ugly and has no friends."

Okay what the hell? "SERIOUSLY? YOU BITCH! You called Noah a fag."

"No I didn't why would I say such a thing?"

"You did do such a thing!"

"Miss. Lake sit down. I'll see you after class. Does someone want to take Miss..."

"Adams, Lisa Adams." she purred. "What a hoe." Jane muttered. I couldn't help but agree.

"Miss. Adams to the nurse."

"Mr. Night? Can't you take me?" Lisa cried.

"I would but I have a class to teach."

"You are so devoted as a teacher." She said with awe in her voice I rolled my eyes. What a bitch.

"I'll take her." Jane said with a wicked smile.

Lisa's eyes got big as she panicked. Jane was known for being a bitch. One who wasn't afraid to hit a hoe. "No I'm good. I'll just wait till the end of class." She said in a rushed voice.

"Okay are you sure?"

"Yes." Then she sat down.

Jane just smiled to herself as I laughed.

"Back to..."Mr. Night began looking at Noah.

"Noah."

"Noah's question, I'm not technically with her. But I've been devoted to loving her only for about eight years now."

All the girls looked hopeful again. "How old are you?" Blake asked.

"I'm 21. I graduated high school at 16."

"So you're like a genius."

"Not really but I am quite smart, now enough about me. Let's go around the room, starting with this beautiful young lady here." He said pointing to Kali, amousy girl with brown hair and doe eyes.

Her face was beat red as she started "I'm Kali. I'm 16. I like to watch movies." She said in a quiet voice.

And then the introduction started. I almost fell asleep until Noah hit me in the rib and I cried out in pain. "Miss. Lake do we have a problem?" Mr. Night asked.

"No. my foot fell asleep." I said lamely.

"Well since you're a little sleepy back there how about you tell us about yourself."

I sighed and pushed my glasses up a little as they were falling off. "I'm Hayley. 16. I like reading and I hate annoying teachers who make me introduce myself."

Every girl gasped. Noah looked like he was going to have a stroke. What I thought? I didn't like this guy. Everyone looked either shocked or mad at me, everyone but Mr. Lake he just smiled.

DING DING DING. The bell went off. I sighed saved by the bell. Thank god. I grabbed my books and started to run out of the class room when I heard Mr. Night call "Miss. Lake I'd like to talk about you behavior in class."

Shit. I waited behind till everyone was out of the class room. Hearing remarks about how I better be careful and watch what I say. Like I really cared what they thought. Once the class was empty I went up to Mr. Night's desk. 'Yes." I asked.

He sighed and looked at me. "Well, Miss, Lake you slapped a girl in the middle of class then disrespected me. What should I do with you?"

"Let me leave?"I asked.

"Nope, detention for a month 3 o'clock till 5. I'll take you home. So you don't have to bother your family."

"A month! That's not fair. Lisa called Noah a fag and you don't even give her a day of detention."

"I didn't hear her say anything therefore I cannot punish her."

"Whatever." I said and stormed out.

"3 o'clock." I heard Mr. Night call.

I hate him.

Chapter 2: My Mate

Logan's POV:

Okay this whole become a teacher things is going to kill me! I blame my father honestly, it's crazy. I'm like what 21? What's the point of this? But I couldn't say no. My father was Alpha, there was no way I refuse his command the moment he made it.

So I guess he just wanted me to, how did he say it? Become more responsible and mature to be more ready to run the pack. There was nothing wrong with the life I was living, screwing random girls, one night stands were the best. But I also have my regulars. Call me a player but that's who I am. I'm in love though, but it's not going to happen. It's been 8 years since I've met her. My mate, my one and only love, my soul mate. I sighed and shook all thoughts of her out of my head. I needed to forget about her, even though it was going to be impossible I needed to try to forget.

I sighed and drove into the parking lot of McKinley High School. For one, I AM a werewolf not some shape shifter. I hate those things. I don't need the full moon to shift, and silver doesn't do shit. But if you did shot me yes I'd bleed and maybe die, depending on where you shoot. I would not survive one through the heart or brain, I mean who would? Werewolves do run in packs and there is an alpha, we do talk in our minds but we can talk to ANYONE we want, werewolf or anything other type of being, whether it's a human or a vampire, but only if they don't block us out, and they can if they were a wear of it.

As I walked into the school I felt suddenly excited. I went from being completely and utterly bored to wanting to be here more than anything. I felt pulled towards an object, like a piece of silver (A/N is it metal or silver, or does it even matter????) to a magnet. I kept walking my pace getting faster and faster till I stopped suddenly smelling the most amazing smell in the world, like caramel, chocolate and vanilla, you'd think that'd smell awful but it really is amazing. I started walking again almost sprinting as I saw her.

The moment I saw her I knew I had to have her. I needed to make her mine. She WAS mine. MY mate. Mine. She was the most beautiful girl I have ever seen. Her wavy black hair flowed perfectly down her back in a waterfall of dark shinny hair. Her face that would have looked plain and boring to the normal eye, but I saw beautiful grey/silver eyes with dark black lashes framing them to perfection. Her lips were full and rosy perfect for kissing. Her body was thin and standing at only about 5'1 her frame was amazing, her body was fantastic. Her glasses were blocking most of her face, why would she do that? She had the most amazing face I had ever seen. It was her, the girl I had seen 8 years ago. It was HER! I finally found her.

I felt myself being pulled towards her, I started to walk her way and as I did I was cut off by some red head. "Hello!" she said in some high picked whiny voice that I found distasteful and annoying.

"Hello," I said politely. "Who are you?"

The girl smiled and started to twirl her hair "I'm Anne McLane. Who are you?" she asked, putting her hand on my chest.

I backed up slowly her hand falling down to her side. "I'm Logan Night, the new biology teacher."

Her eyes started to sparkle. "Oh, I thought you were a bit too old to be a high school student. How old are you?"

"I'm 21." I answered with distain in my voice.

"Oh really? so young?"

"I graduated high school at a young age." I answered looking over her head at my mate. She was now talking with three people. Two were girls, both blonde, but extremely different from one another. The one blonde was tall and thin, blue eyes small nose dressed head to toe in pink, like a regular Barbie doll, once I might have found her attractive but now she doesn't hold a flame to my mate. The other blonde was tall but a bit smaller than the other, her hair had strips of black and blue to them. Her eyes were surrounded with an extreme amount of makeup around them. The boy was tall, about 6'1/6'2, he would have been considered quiet good looking to most girls, I saw him as a rival, and he seemed close with my mate. I saw him say something to her and she laughed, I was so jealous I almost went over there and ripped off his head.

"-and most teachers trust me, so if you ever need anything you can just ask me." Anne said. I just realized that I hadn't been listening to what she just said.

I just smiled said "Thank you." She was saying something when I watched my mate walk away from her friends, having a sensual sway to her walk. I was practically drooling when I said "who's that?" without even thinking, cutting off Anne from whatever she was saying.

"Who?" she asked.

"Her," I said while pointing at my mates retreating figure.

"Why do you want to know about her? she's like a major freak in this school. She doesn't talk to anyone in this school besides Noah and Jane, like she thinks she's better then everyone here."

I felt a sudden wave of anger and jealousy. Anger because of the way she was talking about my mate and jealousy because one of her closest friends was a guy. This Noah guy was one of her good friends, someone she probably hung out with, someone she probably trusted. Just thinking about him and her TOGETHER made me so jealous I wanted to rip his heart out and feed it to the pack. "What's her name?" I asked trying not to snap but it came out cold and angry.

Anne looked startled at the change in my voice. "Her name is Hayley Lake. She's a junior this year."

"Thank you. Now please excuse me, class is going to start soon." I said in a smooth voice.

"No of course! If you need anything just look for me." She said her voice much too enthusiastic for my taste.

I sighed and walked into my class room. In all my years of living I have never in my life seen so many girls that looked the same. The same clothes the same hair color, and even the same annoying giggle. If it weren't for the hope that my mate was in one of my classes I'd kill myself after the afternoon of desperate flirting and annoying banter from these dimwitted girls.

I was totally exhausted by the time 5th period came around, as I was just about to give up all hope about seeing my mate i started so smell that familiar sent of vanilla, caramel, and chocolate. I looked up from my desk and saw her. I was so happy I almost stood up and started to dance for joy. I was so excited I couldn't help myself when I started to grin widely and laugh out loud. I watched her and her two friends go to the back of the room and sat in the back desk by the window.

I felt like a stalker watching her, following her slim figure with my eyes, I was probably drooling, just watching her lick her lips made me want to do dirty things to her after class. It took all my strength not to go to her and do her right in the middle of the class room. Ugh I felt like such a pervert. She was 16 for crying out loud. I've been through this all before. When I saw her by the waterfall, I was 13 and I was just getting used to changing, I was in my wolf form when I smelled her. I ran towards the smell just to see a little girl sitting by the waterfall looking at the water. Her little body that probably wouldn't have stood even up to my chin, her long black wavy hair was in little pig tails, her blue eyes shone with excitement. I felt an over whelming sense of love and the need to protect her. I got scared about those feelings for a little girl I ran away. I remember that night I talked to my dad about it and he explained about the mating process. It took me a couple days to coop with the feelings then I went out to look for her, I spent weeks and months, going on to a year looking for her. Then I gave up looking for her and began to try to forget her, using girls over and over again just trying to forget that one little girl.

The bell rang, calling class to order, snapping me out of my thoughts. I looked at my mate, she was sound asleep, her face looked so peaceful and happy. "Hello class! How was your morning?" I asked.

I heard a chores of good, I looked at my mate she was still sound asleep, oblivious to my love for her and the fact I was staring intently at her, dying for her attention. "Mrs. Rain quiet due to some personal reasons so I guess I'll be your teacher till further notice, I hope you don't mind."

"I don't mind at all." Said a girl towards the back, she looked at me in a seductive way and then winked at me. I shuddered in disgust, don't girls anymore have respect?

I looked to the back of the class again, my mate, was still asleep. I walked towards her desk slowly, I saw her friend, Noah tapping her shoulder trying to wake her up. "What's her name?" I asked Noah, even though I knew it, it'd be weird to address her without truly asking someone who she knew. "Hayley. She hasn't been able to sleep in the past two days, her dad is away on business and her uncle is watching her until he comes back, and she-well she justs been staying up worrying about her dad." I nodded and mentally frowned at his familiar way of addressing her.

"Hayley." I called. I shook her shouldered, I felt a shiver of ecstasy run down my body by just touching her shoulder. I was whipped and she didn't even know it. "Miss. Lake. Please wake up. I do not appreciate you sleeping in my class room."

She slowly started to come to, "You're not a wolf." She said looking at me.

I was shocked, what did she mean. But before I could ask her a question she said "Did I really just say that?"

"Yes you did Miss. Lake."

She looked surprised at my answer then frowned. "Crap did I just say that too?" she said.

I laughed silently, finally understanding her look of surprise, she doesn't think before she talks. "Yes you did. Anyways please do not fall asleep again. Pay attention." I said trying to sound stern. She just nodded and frowned. "Okay now that I have everyone attention," I continued looking at Hayley. She blushed, it was so cute. I just wanted to eat her up! I sounded like an old grandma, ugh. "I'm Mr. Night. Yes that's my real last name. I was born with it. Since it's my first day I just want to take the time to get to know you. And answer your questions about me."

A Barbie blonde raised her hand, how many blondes could there seriously be in this school? "Yes Miss..."

"Amy." She said sweetly.

"Yes Amy what's your question."

"Are you single?" I think that was the 3rd time I heard that in one day. Even if I was their age, why in gods name would I have any interest in these boring Barbie bimbos.

"Yes I am. But I have someone I love very much." I answered looking at Hayley, she shifted uncomfortably under the intensity of my stare.

"Oh..." she said.

The little fuck head raised his hand next. What did he want? "How long have you two been going out?"I was a little surprised at the question. Why would he want to know?

I was just about to answer when I heard a girl in the back say. "Shut up fag." I watched at Noah blushed and shrunk in his seat ashamed. He was gay? I thought? Gay! YES!! That means him and my mate aren't going out! I didn't have any competition. I was so happy I almost started to jump up and down, for the 3rd time in one day, there was seriously something wrong with me now. I was about to answer Noah's question when I saw my little mate get up and walk over to the girl who called Noah a fag and slapped her in the face. I was a little shocked that she did that, but it was hot as hell.

The girl started to cry, she got up and ran to me, clinging to me like a child. It took every ounce of my control not to push her off me in disgust. "Why did she do that? I was just sitting there and she came up and slapped me. That was so mean! You know, Hayley's always been jealous of me I'm beautiful and guys like me while she's so ugly and has no friends." UGLY? SHE DARED CALL MY MATE UGLY!

"SERIOUSLY? YOU BITCH! You called Noah a fag." My mate screamed.

"No I didn't why would I say such a thing?" the slut answered.

"You did do such a thing!"

I had to stop this before Hayley got into a bigger amount of trouble, something that I couldn't help her out of. "Miss. Lake sit down. I'll see you after class. Does someone want to take Miss..." I said drifting off not knowing the name of the stupid girl that was clinging on to me.

"Adams, Lisa Adams." she purred. "What a hoe."Hayley's other friend said under her breathe.

"Miss. Adams to the nurse."

"Mr. Night? Can't you take me?" Lisa whined, her voice was so annoying.

"I would but I have a class to teach." I said, smoothly as I could, trying to keep the disgust out of my voice.

"You are so devoted as a teacher."

"I'll take her."Hayley's friend said, her smile was sort of sadistic.

"No I'm good. I'll just wait till the end of class." She said in a rushed voice.

"Okay are you sure?" I asked suddenly confused.

"Yes." Then she sat down.

"Back to..." I said gesturing at Noah, I technically shouldn't know his name so I didn't say it.

"Noah."

"Noah's question, I'm not technically with her. But I've been devoted to loving her only for about eight years now."

"How old are you?" asked the blonde girl that was talking to my angel before.

"I'm 21. I graduated high school at 16."

"So you're like a genius."

"Not really but I am quite smart. Enough about me. Let's go around the room. Starting with this beautiful young lady here."

And then the introduction started, I sort of tuned everything out, running on automatic. My mind drifting to my mate, she was perfect in every way. But how was I going to get close to her? she was my student I was her teacher. It just wasn't moral. But neither was the age difference. UGH! I WAS A PERVERT! While I was mentally panicking I heard a cry of pain. I looked up, it was my mate. She was rubbing her side. Was she okay? Was she hurt? What could I do to help? "Miss. Lake do we have a problem?" I asked, trying to keep the overwhelming feeling of concern out of my voice, that would scare her.

"No. my foot fell asleep." She said, but she was lying. But she seemed fine. I sighed in relief.

"Well since you're a little sleepy back there how about you tell us about yourself." I asked a little too excited to hear about her.

She sighed and adjusted her glasses. "I'm Hayley. 16. I like reading and I hate annoying teachers who make me introduce myself." I really like this girl I thought.

DING DING DING. The bell went off. I frowned, upset that I just lost my time with her. "Miss. Lake I'd like to talk about you behavior in class." I said, trying desperately to keep her with me, if only for awhile.

"Yes." She asked, apprehensively and nervous.

"Well, Miss, Lake you slapped a girl in the middle of class then disrespected me. What should I do with you?" I asked. Thinking of all the things I could do with her.

"Let me leave?" she said, like hell I was.

"No. Detention for a month. 3-5. I'll take you home. So you don't have to bother your family." I said proud that I came up with an idea to get to be with her without being a stalker freak.

"a month! That's not fair. Lisa called Noah a fag and you don't even give her a days detention." She cried upset. I felt bad that I was making her mad but I needed her around me, and id do anything to keep her near me.

"I didn't hear her say anything therefore I cannot punish her." I said lying smoothly.

"Whatever." She said and stormed out.

"3 o'clock." I called, smiling to myself while I listened to her mumble a string of profanities. I couldn't wait till 3.

okayy so i'm not going to do this whole girls pov then go back and redue to be the guys pov again. i only did it this time b.c you needed to know a bit about logan...ughhh....i'm sucha sucky writer...anyways next time its gonna be Hayley's pov...i think...idk.... :(blah...breaks almost over, boo! SCHOOL MUST DIE!

Chapter 3: Detention

C hapter 3

Hayleys pov:

I walked out of bio swearing under my breath! He was just so annoying! if I would have been a cartoon character my face would be red and smoke would be coming out of my ears. I mean I probably shouldn't have slapped lisa in class, that wasn't the best judgment call I have ever made. But seriously? A whole month for two hours a day? What the hell was he thinking? Couldn't he just have suspended me for a week or given me iss(in school suspension) I swear if I ever saw him outside school I'll strangle him. I don't care about the jail time. It'd be worth it.

I sighed I really had to stop thinking illegal things. It'll get me in trouble one of these days... I walked to my locker ignoring the angry remarks for mr.nights fans. How the heck could he have gotten such a huge fan base already? He's been here what? 4 hours? Crazy mother effin jerk. "woah," Jane said to me as I opened my locker putting my things away to go to lunch. "I never would have thought you'd ever hit someone. Ever. Then disrespect a teacher in class. I was shocked you even said anything. That alone was astounding." noah nodded in agreement.

"well for one Lisa needs to seriously shut up! I have had enough of her homophobic attitude. It was seriously ticking me off. She's just ticked at you for turning her down at homecoming freshman year. Secondly, mr.night just pisses me off. He's sucha self-centered jerk. He gave me a month of detention for 2 hours after school! Why the heck would he do that! I wanna smack him!"

"such violence! I'd jump at the chance to stay after school with him!" Noah said.

"well I would let you take my place but I think he'd realize it wasn't me."

"no way! I wouldn't have ever guest that." Noah said in mock horror.

I smiled and said "come on let's get to lunch I'm starving." Jane and Noah nodded in agreement as we made our way to lunch talking about useless stuff and the latest drama in school. "hey Hayley?" jane asked.

"yea..."

"when's your dad getting back?"

I frowned. Ever since my mom died my dad hasn't been the same. He is almost never home always on a buissness trip, he can barely look me in the eyes anymore. But I know it kills him. Mom meant everything to dad. And I look so much like her it's hard for him to be around me and not think about mom. But even though I understand it kills me. When I needed him the most he wasn't there. When it happened my daddy wasn't there. Mu uncles practically been raising me since I was eight. And as much as I loved my uncle he still wasn't my dad. "I don't know." I said truthfully.

"oh," Jane sad sympathetic.

Noah frowned at the awkwardness and then smiled. "sleepover!!!!" he said.

"what?" I asked confused.

"sleepover Saturday. Your house. It'll be fun. Well get Chinese and those really weird saw movies you like so much."

"I don't know..."

"don't say no! Even if you did me and Jane will come I've anyways right Jane?"

Jane nodded and said "yep! Plus your uncle will agree with us that you need company."

I sighed. There was no fighting with them. "fine..."

"yes!" Jane and Noah said at the same time. It really freaked me out when they did that. And they did that a lot. You'd think they were siblings of you didn't already know them.

We made our way into the cafeteria and got in the lunch line. Yuck, it was chicken. And normally I like chicken but it was school food. I debated either getting that or risk food poisoning or just getting the overpriced pizza. I could have just not eaten but I needed my food. I was a growing girl. I looked at the chicken one more time and frowned. "Pizza here I come. You better be worth the extra $1.50." I said mumbling under my breath.

I heard a quiet laughter coming from the side of me. I looked to see who it was and it was none other than the guy who makes my life living hell. Mr Night. "What do you want?" I said angrily. Okay so I knew this was not the way you talked to teachers but he ticked me off so much. And I really had no idea why. It was probably because I felt so awkward around him all the time.

"nothing. You're just so cute talking to yourself."

That was not what I was expecting to come out of his mouth. "oh..." I said lamely.

He just smiled grabbed his pizza and said "don't be late. 3'o clock. If your even a minute late I'm adding on another week." I just gaped at him as he walked away. What a dick! I thought. I really did not like him.

The rest of the day went by slowly. I honestly felt like I was moving through maple syrup the whole day. During 8th period gym I got hit in the head with a volleyball and had to go to the nurse. I had such a bad head ache I wanted to go home. But then I remember mr.nights warning about being late. If he added on for being late I could just image what he'd do if I didn't show up.

So right at 3 after the bell rang I made my way to the science lab and walked in right on time. "I'm here." I said as I walked through the door. But what I saw I was not ready to see. I saw miss.kelly almost on top of mr. Night. It look like they were making out. But only mr.night looked freaked out and disgusted. While miss.Kelly looked desperate..."I'll just leave..." I said starting to back out the door.

"no!" mr.night said looking terrified, like someone just killed his cat. "don't go. Please stay." he said. His voice desperate. What the hell?

Miss.Kelly looked flustered and said "yes miss.lake stay. I'll just be leaving now." she walked by me quickly and gave me a dirty look as she passed by me. Ugh I hate every single freaking girl in this school.(besides Jane duh!:) Even the teachers. Was it a rule to be a bitch here?

"well..." I said awkwardly.

Mr.night just smiled at me and said "is every girl in this school that desperate?"

I laughed and said "pretty much. Miss.Kelly huh? Way to be a man slut." shit. I shouldn't have said that too him. He's my teacher. Not a normal guy. I could get in trouble for that.

He just looked at me his eyes hurt, but when he realized i was joking he looked at me with mock horror and said "me a man slut! If I may, she jumped me first!"

I just laughed in relief. "so what do you want me to do?"

He just looked at me strangely for a second then seemed to remember where he was and who he was. "well," he started. "I was looking at your grades you have a 63 in this class. Which you should know by now is a failing grade."

"yea your point..." what was he getting at.

"well I think during this month we have together I would tutor you to help you get your grades up."

"seriously?" I asked, shocked.

"yes. But the first hour you have to clean the room. Dust the shelves, wash the floor and clean the desks, organize the books and some papers." he said with a smirk. And just when I thought he was human. "okay?"

I just frowned and said "whatever."

Mr. Night smiled and said "start with the floors."

I groaned. I swear I was going to throw up on him.(a/n it's something I tend to say when I'm mad and want someone to suffer. I think being thrown up on is the worst thing that could happen to you...) i grabbed a bucket and mop from the supply closet. I went to the sink and filled it with hot water. I put my ear buds in my ear and played the first thing that was on my playlist. It turned out to be avril's one of those girls. As I washed the floors I got really into my music and started to sing along stupidly. Then I started to dance with the mop while singing. I was completely into ii forgot where I was until I heard laughter. And not just giggling, like rolling on the floor dying of laughter. I looked at him and frowned. "mr.nnight!" I yelled complaining. But he didn't even hear me he was laughing so hard. "hey!" I said getting mad. I was so embarrassed by now my face would have been a great color for a tomatoes.

He just looked at me and started to laugh harder. "I'm-" he started to say "sorry- it's just that" fits of laughter. "it was just so-" still laughing. "funny. I mean-" he couldn't even finish he's sentence he was laughing so much.

"stop!" I said tying not to laugh myself. It was pretty funny.

He just laughed. And finally I gave in and we were both cracking up laughing. When we finally calmed down he looked at me and said "you were so cute singing and dancing i could help but laugh. It was so funny."

For some reason i was okay with him saying that. I just smirked. "you're mean!"

"I am not! You can't blame me! It was jus so funny!" he protested.

"whatever! You owe me!"

"for what?!"

"for making fun of me! That wasn't nice it hurt my feelings!" I said in mock anger.

He just smiled a heart breaking smile and said "fine. I'll cut his detention short and take you out to eat."

Okay call me fat but the moment he said food I didn't care that I hated him. I'll take free food anyway. "really?"

He just smiled wider. He looked almost excited. "yes. Where do u wanna go?"

I thought for a minute. I was really in the mood for a big mac. "mcdonalds!"

"you look like an overly medicated four year old right you know that right."

I just frowned and said "meanie!"

He laughed grabbed his stuff and said "come on." I nodded and grabbed my book bag. We made our way out of the school and to the parking lot. He had a really nice car. I don't know the model or the make, I'm not a car person, but I didn't have to be one to know this car probably cost a small fortune. What the heck was he doing as teacher. He obviously didn't need the money.

"mr night?" I asked.

"call me Logan."

"huh? Whose Logan?"

He laughed slightly and pointed to himself. "I'm Logan. That's my name. Call me Logan when we are outside of school. Mr.night makes me feel old, like my father."

"you are old mr- Logan."

"I'm 21! How's that old?"

"your older than me therefore you are old." I pointed out.

He frowned a little at my comment. He almost looked sad. "whatever. What was your question?"

I forgot about that. "oh yea. Why r you a teacher? With this car you obviously don't need the money."

He looked at me thoughtfully out of the corner of his eye and said. "my dad wanted to teach me responsibility. so he sent me here. My uncle is the principle of the school so he gave me the job.

"aren't you mad?"

He just turned and smiled at me "I was but not anymore."

Then he turned back to the road and continued driving. What did he mean by that? Stupid arrogant jerk face. I thought.

Chapter 4: She's Human

Chapter four

Logan's POV:)

I watched her from the corner of my eye for her response. She pretty much looks unaffected by my words. I mean why should she have anything to respond too? Even though I knew I was talking about her being the reason I wasn't mad about coming here. I know I shouldn't have said that considering I was her teacher and she was my student, but no matter how much I try to deny it, she was my mate and I loved her like nothing else in this world. She was part of me and if she wasn't with me I was only half a man. The whole is greater than the sum of its part(a/n geometry bitch ;)

The rest of the drive to mcdonalds was quiet. She sat there in thought and I was just happy to have her by me. Just her presence made me smile. We went through the drive threw and I turned to her and said "what do you want?"

Without a moment to think she said "big mac! Make it a large, with a coke and two BBQ sauces!"

Okay she was the size of my arm how could she eat that much? "Okay," I repeated her order and then road up to the first window. "Aren't you going to get anything mr.nig-Logan?" she asked.

It took me a minute to answer I was to caught up on how she said my name... "naw, I'm not hungry."

"okay..." she said.

She was just cute! We got the food, paid for it and then parked in the parking lot. I gave her, her food and watched her eat. Call me a creep but that's the only reason I didn't get food. I wanted to watch how my little mate ate...I was getting weirder and weirder.

She was stuffing her face like she hadn't eaten in days, it was the cutest thing I've ever seen. I was smirking as I watched her dip her fry into the BBQ sauce. THAT was gross...yet endearing. "ew," I said. "Why do you do that? Those fries are good just the way they are."

She smirked and said "No, dipping you're fries into BBQ sauce is completely normal. A lot of people do that."

"No they don't."

"Yea...what do you do? Eat them plan or dip them in a milk shake?"I just smiled and waited for her to put one and one together. "Ew you do not?"

"What do I do?" I said innocently.

"You don't."

"I don't what?"

"YOU DIP YOUR FRIES INTO MILK SHAKES?! THAT'S JUST DISGUSTING?" she screamed in horror. "What's next? You dunk your Oreos in milk?" I just smiled. She frowned, "You do don't you?"

"Yup. " I said popping my p.

"Dude, that's just gross." She said.

I was just about to say something when her phone went off. Her ring tone was Space Bound by Eminem, I never would have pegged her for an Eminem fan. "Hello?" she said.

I listened closer to hear what the other person on the other end said. "Hayley Marie Lake! Get your butt home right now. It's almost 5, you should have been home by 3! Do you have any idea about how worried I am? I thought you got kidnapped or ran over, or worse! MURREDER!"

"Shit." Hayley murmur, so low I could barely hear it. "Sorry Uncle David. I forgot to call you! I have detention for the next month 3-5."

I heard the guy sigh on the other line. "Hayley, I know I'm not your dad but I didn't think I was doing that bad of a job raising you so you would lash out at society."

"Oh stop being such a drama queen."

"Well! Tell me! What did you do?"

"I hit a girl in class..."

"What? HAYLEY!"

"Well she was being a bitch towards Noah!"

"Hey! Language young lady! And well it doesn't mean you hit her, and if you have to do it out of class!" I laughed silently. I really liked her uncle.

"Well thanks for the tip. I'll be home in 20."

"Okay, be careful kid."

"Yea. Bye." She said and hung up. "You know," she said turning to me, "Ease dropping killed that cat."

"Yea, but I'm not a cat." I said sweetly. "I'm a dog."I said ironically.

"Yea okay, sure I bet there's some sorta saying about dogs to?"

"Well my inner dog has a big ego." I said, it was almost scary to me how much I was actually telling her about me without truly telling her.

"Wow, you have more issues then I do." She said thumping me on the head.

I smiled. At least she was comfortable around me, I was almost overly happy about her being able to act like her, not my student, but a friend. "Now take me home!" she commanded. She'd be a good alpha's mate.

Even though my wolf didn't like being told what to do, she was my mate, my baby, my angel, my love, she could tell me to do anything and I would comply without a second thought. "Yes sir! Where to?" she gave me the address and I nodded and started that way. We were driving only about 5 minutes when she reached for the radio, I looked at her and her hand stopped. "Can I put some music on?" she asked.

I smiled and nodded. She smiled back and turned it on. She fiddled with it for awhile till she found the station she wanted. 'I write sins not tragedies' by panic at the disco was playing. I looked at Hayley, her smiled was brilliant, she was so beautiful, I watched as her perfect pink lips mouthed the words, I couldn't help but want to kiss those beautiful lips, caress her lovely body. As I drove to her house I couldn't help but picture her in my bed, panting my name, shit. I really need to stop thinking these things. "Hey! MR.NIGHT? HELLO?" Hayley's voice said "You in there? You missed the turn back there."

"Sorry," I mumbled, then realized what she called me. "What did you just call me? Didn't I just tell you to call me Logan when we were outside school?"

"Yea, but,"

"But what?"

"It's just awkward if I call you by your first name, you're my teacher so..."

"So what? When we aren't in class I'm not technically your teacher at the moment."

"Yea you are. We might not be in class but you're still my teacher."

I frowned, this girl really had a way to make me upset. My heart hurt that the thought she only saw me as her teacher. I mean I didn't really expect her to like me right away but maybe she could think of me as a friend?

"Right here!" she screamed, bringing me out of my thoughts. I turned into the driveway of a good sized light blue house. It had two floors and a white door. An older white man was standing in front of the door his arms crossed. His expression turned from worry to relief the moment he saw Hayley in the front seat. He looked about 45, his brown hair and blue eyes resembled that of Hayley's, was that her dad or her uncle. Curiosity overwhelmed me and I reached into his mind.

Should I tell her father? I mean even if I tell him would he care? What a dick, I mean sure he's my brother but he should try to care about his daughter a little more. I'm more of a father to Hayley then he was. I get that his wife died and Hayley looks just like her but Hayley needed him. After what happened, stop thinking about it David. Stop! Hayley asked you to put this behind you, so do it. Ugh. Hayley, your uncle is worried.

I left his mind and looked at him again. What was he talking about? What happened? Either way, what type of father wasn't there for his daughter. I looked up at Hayley's uncle he was looking at me with curiosity, Hayley grabbed her book bag that was at her feet and got out of the car and said "Thank you Mr. Night see you tomorrow." She smiled sweetly and closed the door. She was an idiot if she thinks I was just going to leave now.

"Hayley!" her uncle said and hugged her as she tried to walk through the door. "I was so worried! My little girl didn't come home when she was supposed to! What do you think daddy would do without her little girl!" he said hugging her tightly.

What? I thought he was her uncle? "Uncle, you aren't my dad." Hayley said.

Hurt flashed across his face. "But I've been with you since you were eight! You are practically my daughter! I love you like one." He said and gave her the puppy dog face.

She sighed in annoyance and was just about to say something when she noticed that I was still there. She called out from the doorway. "WHAT DO YOU WANT?"

I smiled and got out of the car and walked up to them. "Hello, I'm Logan Night." I told her uncle and raised my hand to shake his.

Her uncle gave me a hard look and reached out his hand to meet mine, he squeezed with too much force, but I was a werewolf it wasn't going to do much to me. "What are you doing with my little girl?" he was a dotting uncle I could tell.

"I'm her teacher. I drove her home from school."

"Are you the teacher who gave her detention?"

Well I guess her uncle isn't going to like me very much. "Yes..."

"You know what? My little girl is a good girl, she has never done anything wrong in her life. When I'm sick she takes time out of her day to take care of me. She does the cooking and the cleaning around here. So if you think you were justified at all for giving my little gir-ouch! Hay-Ley! What was that for?"

"Uncle, get inside or no dinner."

"But Hayley! I was just trying to help."

Hayley just gave him a stern look and he nodded. Once he was inside I smiled at her. "You're uncle sure is something."

"Yea, I love him, but he is rather different."

"Yea, why is your uncle taking care of you, and not your parents?"

"My mom died when I was eight, and my dad was so affected about it he has a hard time looking at me. But it's okay, I understand." She looked at me with a confident smile, but you could see the hurt in her eyes. I just wanted to hold her in my arms and hold her till all the pain went away. "Well, I you didn't need anything you should leave, I got to talk to my uncle about his behavior today."

I just smiled and said "Well you're lucky I'm such a great guy or I'd give you an f on your next test because of your uncle's behavior." Even though I knew it was annoy her, she was just so cute when she got mad.

Her face turned red and she opened the door and slammed it in my face without even saying goodbye. I still had a stupid smirk on my face as I drove home.

I pulled into my driveway and saw that little Julie and Owen were playing soccer in the front yard. "LOGAN! HEY!" they both cried and ran up to greet me. I smiled at my eight year old cousin and her friend and said "Hey guys. Mind if I play?"

"Sure, but let us finish this one. You go inside and find someone else to be on your team." I smiled and walked in the door. I was greeted by all my family and pack. "how was your first day Logan?" an annoying voice asked from behind me.

I turned to see Jasmine, one of my...well...fuck buddies...but now that I meet Hayley I didn't need her. I smiled and said honestly "It was the best day ever. I meet the sweetest girl."

"Wouldn't she be a student? Isn't that illegal?" Jasmine sneered.

"Sure, but she'll be graduating in a year. I can wait."

"She isn't even one of us, she's only a puny human, and a child. You'll realize that you need me when you find out how much of a kid she really is."

By now I was pissed. How could she talk about my mate like that? "Shut up Jasmine," I said dangerously. She backed off, listening to my command. I was still angry so I walked away from her before I could hurt her. "Hey Logan! Buddy! How was hell?" Craig my best friend asked.

"I found my mate." I said.

"REALLY! OH LOGAN I'M SO HAPPY FOR YOU!" I turned and saw my mom running towards me and enveloping me into a big hug. "Oh! Is she a teacher? How old is she? Does she like shopping? We need more girls around here! I've always wanted a daughter! What pack is she from? I hope she isn't married with children already."

"Mom mom mom, slow down please. She isn't a teacher."

"Oh really?" my mom said her face turning concerned. "She isn't-oh Logan."

"Yea she's a student, she a junior this year."

"Oh-well, her pack will understand," I gave her a look "She's human."

" Yup."

My dad looked at me upset, my mom looked at me with same face as my dad. I saw jasmine smile and Craig just started to laugh. "Sucks for you buddy."

Thanks Craig, thanks...my life just got a little more complicated.

boring for now, but it's gonna get more interesting soon.

Chapter 5: Yes I'm Stalking My Mate, You Have A Problem With That?

Logan's POV: (remember...you really should read the top it's important information you need to know)

I was going to die. How much more pain could my body handle before I pass out? God, why does this have to happen to me? Haven't I been a good person? Sure I've slept with...like...48 girls, maybe many more. I was so piss drunk half the time I probably left out a few dozen... And yea sure, I've hurt a few people. And yes just two hours ago I swore at my little cousin for kicking my butt in soccer, but seriously? This pain was so unbearable I wanted to die. But why does this have to happen to me? I stared at the clock: it was only 10:00pm, I saw my mate just five hours ago and already I was going through withdrawal. I needed her by my side, to smile at me, to laugh with me, to just exist. But I also desperately craved her presence. I needed her.

I needed a distraction. So I thought of when I went over to my parent's house after I dropped off Hayley off. I thought back. After Craig LAUGHED at me, I talked to my parents about Hayley. They weren't nearly as concerned as I was about her being my student, to them that was the minor detail, one that could be fixed in just a year and a half. But they were worried that she was human. They had no prejudice about humans, well Jasmine did, but other than her no one really had anything against humans, but a human as a mate. That was completely different. It happened, but very rarely. But every werewolf and human mating process was terminated by the werewolves' very pack. But me being Alpha, it made it so much worse.

Then I got hit by a terrifying reality. HAYLEY COULD BE KILLED BY SOMEONE IN MY VERY OWN PACK! Now not only did I have to worry about her getting sick, being in a car accident, tripping and hurting herself, but now I have to worry about her being KILLED by werewolves, MY werewolves. It was almost as bad as humans. Thinking about her getting hurt or murdered by ANYONE just got my blood pumping. I heard a growl in the back of my throat. I felt my teeth start to grow and sharpen, my fingers grew long and my nails got long and sharp, clawing ready for the kill. I finally snapped. I turned. I felt my bones start to readjust and my body begin to shake. Now in my wolf form I jumped out of the open window and fell four stories from my apartment.

My body knew where I was going to go before my mind did. I was going to Hayley's house. I ran as fast as I could. I ran through the dark streets, too fast for the normal human eye to see me. I was just a block away until I felt another's presence. I stopped and turned around. I saw a white werewolf, small compared to the average wolf, but don't let that fool you. This wolf was the best fighter we had. Marcy was a tiny girl, actually shockingly as a human, she was even smaller then Hayley.

'What are you doing here?' I asked

'What are YOU doing here?' She countered.

'That's my business. Just answer me!' I commanded I knew she couldn't avoid my question now. What are you doing here?

I saw her roll her eyes. 'I'm here for myself alpha's son'. She answered in respect.

'Where are you going?' I asked. Her home, where my parents lived was at least 45 miles away. Why would she be all the way out here?

'Alpha's son, I have no intention on hurting your mate, please respect my need for privacy.'

I looked at her, Macy was once a close friend, but as we grew older we grew apart. I had to admit I missed her friendship. She always knew what to say. I should give her her freedom. 'Fine, but you come near my mate I will not hesitate to kill you.'

'I wouldn't expect anything less Logan.' She said with a smile in her voice, saying she remembered our old friendship.

'Go' I said. And she did, she ran her body disappearing into the woods.

I sighed and turned back to run to my mates house. When I got there I went to the side of the house and saw that one window was open. The lights were off and I listened, the house seemed asleep. I turned back into my human form. I listened again, I heard two heart beats, and two people breathing. Both people breath seemed pretty stable, consistent, both were sleeping. I sighed in relief. I scaled the wall and climbed into the window. I was instantly overwhelmed with the sweet, addicting smell of vanilla, chocolate and caramel. I was in HER room. My angel, my baby, my mate, was sound asleep in this room. I looked around, the walls were painted light blue, like the color of her eyes I noticed. Her room was very small, it had only enough room for a small twin bed a desk and a bookshelf. There were two doors, one I assumed lead to a bathroom and the other a closet. There were books EVERYWHERE, stacked up on the desk, they FILLED the bookshelves, on the floor and they lined the walls. I picked up on book closest to me, it was Frankenstein by Mary Shelly.

"Ummm..." I turned towards the little bed were my mate laid. If she woke up I would be screwed. How would I explain? Hayley, hey, I'm in your room because I needed to see you like the obsessed stalker I am, and why am I naked you ask? Well I'm a werewolf, and I ran here in my wolf form and I didn't have any clothes with me. How would she take that? And I'm here teacher, which would be even creepier. I waited still and unmoving, ready to jump back out the window if I had to. But she just rolled over and sighed. I sighed in relief and moved over to her bed and brushed some of the hair out of her face. She was breath taking, she looked like an angel. I loved her so much it broke my heart. I just looked at her until she rolled over to the other side of the bed. I looked at the empty space next to her body on the bed. It looked inviting. I couldn't could I? Oh well, I convinced myself, I'll just be sleeping there for safety precautions. I slipped myself next to her body, I brought the covers over my body and laid next to her. I rolled over on my one side just so I could stare at her sweet face. I was shocked when I saw her move closer to me and cuddle up to my body. She hugged me to her and sighed. I stopped breathing. She had no signs of waking up anytime so. So I got myself comfortable and feel asleep next to her.

I woke up early the next morning, it was around 4 in the morning according to the sun. I sighed, I knew I had to leave her before she woke up and discovered her teacher in her bed, naked. I laughed silently to myself, imagining her embarrassment and rage. She was just too cute. I waited for another hour and I slipped out of her grasp and left through the window. I smiled all the way home.

---

i wasnt gonna upload today, but i was so happy i got 6 comments i sort of just did...??? it was sort of just an extra chapter anyways, this chapter was only written for my enjoyment, it wasn't part of the original story....until now....

COMMENT AND VOTE PLEASE?

Chapter 6: Meeting The Wolf

Hayley's POV:

I sighed and rolled over in my bed. I peeled my eyes open and looked at the clock in annoyance. I had to get up. It was 5:30 and if I didn't get ready now I'd be dead. I got up and walked to my bathroom. I stripped down out of my clothes and jumped into the warm comforting shower, man did I love my shower. It was always warm and inviting. Only when it got mad did it ever trip me.

Once I was done I jumped out of the shower and ran to my towel. It was too cold for it to be March. When I walked out of the door I saw it. It hit me like a ton of bricks. I saw my only love. The one thing that comforted me. And the bitch that stood in my way.

My bed! Oh how I love you. Damned alarm clock, screw you! It's your fault for not letting me be with it.

I sighed at my stupidity and grab a pair of jean shorts, a baggy old linkin park t-shirt, my shoe and I put my oversized glasses on my face. I was ready to face another day of hell. God I hated high school.

I ran out of the house five minutes later with a goodbye to my uncle and a strawberry pop tart. I started walking down the street listening to my iPod and day dreamed. I got to Seneca street and went down a small road then I walked into the woods. This was my own little short cut to school. I always loved the woods. It was like my own safe haven. It made me feel normal again. Like it never happened. Like he never took my innocence away. He had no right. Yet he took my childhood. I almost screamed in frustration when I heard a rustle in the bushes. I paused and turned around. I saw the most beautiful big blue eyes. I knew in my subconscious I should have been afraid. But I wasn't those eyes were so calming. How could I be scared? I walked over to the bush and a huge black wolf appeared out of the trees and branches. It was taller than me. I just continued to look into its eye, they are fascinating, filled with warmth kindness and love. I never know wolfs could have emotions.

The wolf looked almost scared, like it was worried about something. I walked close, it bent its head for me to touch its head. It sort of smiled...could a wolf smile. I petted it head some more and it seemed to sigh. What an odd wolf. I took out my phone to take a picture of it when I noticed the time, 7:20. Shit school starts in 10 minutes.

"Sorry," I said to the wolf, "I have to go! I'll see you later maybe?" then ran off. Was that wolf a dream? I questioned it the whole way to school. How was it so big? Why didn't it run off when it saw me? Why didn't it kill me? So many questions all of which I had no answer to. I pushed it out of my mind when I got to school.

"Hayley Lake! Why in god's name are you so late?" Jane said as I got to my locker.

"Ummm took a short cut, but I got distracted on the way." I said thinking about that beautiful wolf.

"Well next time you get distracted text one of us! We were worried." Noah said his voice sounded distressed.

"Okay," I said with a smile. "Hey are there wolves in this area?"

"No, coyotes, bears maybe, but no wolves. Why do you ask?"

"No reason, just asking."

"Okay....?" Noah said confused.

"Don't worry about it!" I laughed and smiled. Maybe I'm losing it?

Logan's pov:

Shit shit shit shit shit. Could I be anymore stupid? I was supposed to be a genius! But I guess they were wrong. I was so stupid.

After I got home from Hayley's I went back to my apartment got dressed and went to the school. I had some tests I neglected to grade for a month ago in which Mrs. Rain didn't grade. So I was stuck doing the job. But while grading my mind was...well in the gutter should I saying polite pg terms. All last night I had felt her rub against me. And I was naked. Do the math. So after 10 minutes of unsuccessful grading I went out back behind the school stripped down and shifted. I needed a walk to clear my mind. Then I came across that all too familiar sent of vanilla chocolate and caramel. I followed the sent out of instinct and out of need. I need her. I saw her tiny figure walk through the trees on her way to school. I followed her and then I made a mistake. My angels face looked so sad and distressed that I moved to comfort her without thinking about it and

I made a sound. And you would think it wouldn't be such a big thing but it was. She wiped around and saw me. I could've run. I should've run. But I didn't. I stepped out on the path. She looked so beautiful I didn't even use my common sense. She was perfect, her long black hair was blowing in the wind her blue eyes looked at me curiously. I loved her, and she wouldn't know. She couldn't know. It would be dangerous for her. It hurt me like hell to know I could never have her.

But after a bit my logic came back and I looked at her, shit would she run away? Would she scream? She walked up to me slowly and cautiously. She reached her hand out and she petted me slowly. I sighed in contentment. Trying to ignore my wolf, he wanted her, he needed her. He wanted to make her his before someone else took her. I want her. Was the only thing that ran through my head. I tried to ignore it. I really did. I was just finally going to give into my instincts when she took out her phone and looked panicked. She looked at me her phone me the school and said, "Sorry, I have to go! I'll see you later maybe?" than she ran off in a hurry. I just watched her leave me, fighting my inner self to stay put and not chase her down.

And now here I am. In class it was 3rd period 2 more periods till I saw my mate. I chanted in my head 2 more periods over and over again. I was getting pathetic.

I went through two periods and it was finally 5th! I waited in class during the 10 minute break when there was a knock on my door. "Come in." I called.

"So this is where you have been sentenced to hell." Shit I thought. Great, just what I needed, I thought. And I thought today was going to be a good day.

Hayley's POV:

"Come on Hayley! You can't honestly tell me this isn't something you are excited about." Jane whined.

"Jane I honestly don't care. I'm sorry." I said in pure annoyance.

"But I mean seriously! HE LET YOU BORROW A PENCIL!" Jane screamed. She was over excited that THE Kevin Baker lent me his pencil in 4th period. "He's popular and sexy and HE noticed that you didn't have a pencil and HE asked you if YOU wanted to use his. HE talked to you first not the other way around! HE noticed you! Aren't you excited? I heard him talking about you after 3rd period yesterday, when Blake was making fun of you he said 'Shut up Blake, you don't even know her. You can't really say those things about her. She seems really nice and she isn't that bad looking if you get rid of the glasses.' He stood up for you when everyone else was laughing."

"Jane I really don't care." I said in annoyance. Kevin was my next door neighbor. We used to be friends in like what 4th grade, he was always really nice, to everyone. He was student body president, the most popular guy in the school and he wasn't a jerk.

"He's uber hot and he noticed you, and you don't care?"

"Nope" I said, uncaringly.

"You are so weird." Jane said.

I just rolled my eyes. "Why is our Hayley so weird now?" Noah said coming out of nowhere.

"THE Kevin Baker, lent her a pencil and she doesn't care. He didn't even ask for it back!" Jane said happily.

"So..."

"I think he might like her!" Jane screamed.

Noah looked at Jane in horror and screamed "NO HE DOESN'T DON'T TALK ABOUT THINGS YOU DON'T KNOW THAT IS 100% TRUE."

Jane looked shocked for a minute then said, "Dude okay, and don't scream at me."

I looked at Noah's face, he looked panicked, guilty, jealous and angry at once. What the hell? "Whatever," he said and huffed away.

"What's up his butt?" Jane asked in annoyance.

"Hey, Jane go to 5th period I'll be there in a minute, I need to get Noah."

"Okay, see ya..." Jane said and walked away.

I ran after Noah, calling out his name. I thought of his panicked face his guilt for yelling at Jane his jealously, he liked Kevin, and from the rest of his facial expressions, Kevin probably liked him back. "NOAH JACOB TABER! YOU STOP THERE!" I screamed. He stopped in his tracks and waited for me.

"Hayley I'm sorry for yelling at Jane it's just-ugh never mind you won't get it." he said his back to me.

"You like him." I said softly. "You like Kevin, don't you? And he likes you?" I asked.

He turned around and said with tears in his eyes, "How did you know?""I'm your best friend silly. How long?"

"Two months. He was my math tutor, and well..."

I smiled at him and laughed, "That's so cute! Why didn't you tell me and Jane?" I asked.

"Because Kevin was worried, he is so confused by this, I didn't want to put any pressure on him to come out. His parents are super strict and well he doesn't want people to know yet. He'll be graduating this year he wanted to wait to come out when he moves away."

"I get it. Don't worry. I won't tell anyone either."

"Thanks Hayley."

"No problem. Let's get to class before Log- I mean Mr. Night bites our heads off." I said and started to walk away fast, my face beat red from embarrassment, I almost just called Mr. Night by his first name, in school. Ugh.

"Hay-ley. Did I just hear what I thought I did? You wanted to call Mr. Night by Log- what?"

I just continued to walk away. "You are hearing things Noah."

"No I wasn't," he said catching up, "What did you started to call him?"

"Nothing,"

"You meant something."

"No."

"Yes,"

"No,"

"Yes."

"No,"

"Yes."

"No,"

"Yes."

"NO I DIDN'T!"

"Sure you didn't princess. You'll tell me later right?"

"Shut up, come on Noah the bell ran like what 5 minutes ago, Mr. Night's gonna shoot our faces off."

"Whatever, you say, but I think he likes you."

"You're on crack."

"Nope." He said as we got to room 666, I mean seriously it must be a sign, The devil's room number was a devil's number. "What are you waiting for?" Noah asked.

"I'm scared." I said.

"Wimp." Noah goaded.

"No I'm not, it's just that-"

"Miss. Lake, Mr. Taber, it's good of you to finally join us." The terrifying voice of Mr. Night said cutting me off, and swinging the door open almost hitting Noah in the face.

"Sorry." I said, flinching back at the intensity of his glare. Noah just stood there and tried not to laugh.

"Get in your seats." He said menacingly with a touch of amusement.

Noah and I walked to the back of the room and sat down. "Way to be Hayley, you just got yourself in major trouble trying to help a dumbass."

"Sorry Jane, I was out of line." Noah said. "Truth is, I'm dating Kevin, and it hurt me to think he was flirting with Hayley,"

Jane just looked shocked and nodded with a tiny smile on her face. "We'll talk later." She mouthed to Noah.

"Wait what do you mean trouble? He didn't say anything." I said in annoyance.

"Yea but look at him he's just glaring at you, and from yesterday he is defiantly not going to let you off the hook. Especially today."

"Why?"

"Well since you both left me alone with 5 minute to spare I came to class early, I saw Mr. Night yelling at some girl, I bet she's his ex girlfriend, they were talking about something like 'You are going to regret this Logan.' And he said 'Shut up Jasmine, we are over. And if you lay a hand on her I'll kill you.' It was pretty intense, when they saw me she just glared at him and said 'We'll talk about this later.' And left."

"Oh." I said. "Was she really pretty?" I asked, why did I care I thought to myself.

"Beautiful, she was gorgeous. I swear, even as a heterosexual female who likes her men, I would tap that."

"Oh.""Be quiet back there! Did you even here a single thing I said in the past minute Miss. Lake?" Mr. Night said.

"No..."

"I want to see you after class."

"But-"

"No buts."

"Yes sir." He smiled and continued class.

"Sorry Hayley," Jane whispered.

I nodded and smiled. I really hate Logan Night.

Logan's POV:

Okay so I felt bad for calling her out in class, but you can't even fathom how worried she had me when she didn't walk into 5th period. I was so worried about her I almost left the classroom to search for her. After my little talk with Jasmine, I thought she was in an empty hallway bleeding to death, and trust me, Jasmine wasn't afraid to do things like that. I almost lost it in class until Jane, Hayley's friend said "Mr. Night, Hayley and Noah will be late, personal issues." I think I should give Jane a hug, I thought, for it was her who gave me the best news in the world.

I was now sitting at my desk staring at my angel like the stalker I was, memorizing every single detail of her face. I reached into her mind a little before to see what she thought about the wolf thing, but I didn't hear anything. Nothing, now I knew how crappy Edward felt in that stupid Twilight movie, it was frustrating. Why couldn't I read her mind? "Mr. Night," a voice said bringing me from my thoughts, "I need some help on this question." I looked up, it was I think her name was Lindsey, she was one of the few girls that hair wasn't blonde.

"Sure what question?"

"Number 9."

"Okay," I said and continued to explain that answer to her question. I was still aware of Hayley's presence in the classroom, I really wanted her. I felt like a sulky four year old. Seriously? What was this girl doing

to me?

Chapter 7: The Kiss In The Bio Room

Chapter seven

Hayley's POV:

Once 5th period was over I waited in my seat for everyone to clear out, just as I had yesterday. If this became a daily occurrence I was going to punch Mr. Night in the face. Once the room was clear I made my way up to the front of the class room. "Hayley."

"Yes Mr. Night."

He looked at me expectantly for a moment, but once he saw I wasn't getting it he said, "We aren't in class, what do you call me?"

"Logan..." I said grudgingly. What was with him and his first name?

He smiled and said, "So why were you late today?"

"Noah had a personal problem." I said. He frowned ever so slightly and nodded. "Why did you just call me and not Noah?"

"Because, this is you're, I think fourth time disturbing my class while it was his first." I frowned and started to complain until he held up his hand for him to continue, "Lunch detention."

"Are you serious?"

"No, I'm lying..." he said slowly, like he was talking to a four year old. "Go get your lunch then come right up here."

I sighed and said, "Yes sir."

"What?"

"Huh?"

"What did you just call me?"

"Yes Logan."

"That's better."

I walked out of the room, swearing just as I had yesterday, at Logan. He was such a jerk. I swear one day I was going to kill him. But there was something about the way he said my name, 'Hayley,' I remembered how he said it. He said my name with love and kindness, like he cared for me.

I shook those ideas out of my head and walked to my locker, Jane and Noah stood there waiting for me. "Hey what did he said again?" Jane asked.

"I have lunch detention." I said in annoyance as we walked to the cafeteria.

"Ha ha, seriously, that sucks." Noah said.

"Well I'm starting to think he has a little crush on you." Jane said out of nowhere.

"What? Where the hell did you get that idea from?" I asked incredulously.

"He only keeps you after school and after class; he wants to see you during lunch. No normal teacher actually does that. And he gives you these moony eyes in class, like he wants to jump you right there and make sweet passionate love to you."

"Oh my god! So I wasn't the only one who sees those looks he gives her? I thought I was just seeing things." Noah said jumping up and down excitedly.

"Hahaha, nope!"

"You two are crazy you do know that right? Okay I need to go ahead, if I'm not there in like ten minutes he'll skin me alive." Jane and Noah gave each other a look and smiled. They were losing it. I wonder if I should get them a therapist. I ran to the lunch line grabbing a piece of pizza and a power-aid and then continued to bump into Jace Carson (Thanks book7 :), the quarterback of the football team, who then dropped all his food on the floor. "Shit watch it!" He said.

"Sorry." I said quietly.

He looked at me and frowned, "Whatever just be careful next time."

"I'll buy you another lunch." I said.

He smiled at me, his brown eyes seems to shine "No thanks though. Sorry for yelling at you before, my girlfriend just broke up with me so I've been in a bad mood."

"Oh sorry about that."

"It's fine. Hey do you want to sit with me at lunch Hayley?"

"How do you know my name?"

"We've been in the same classes together since 4th grade. You lent me your color pencils in 5th grade when I didn't have any."

I didn't remember this. "Oh, ha, ha thanks for the offer but I have lunch detention." Then I remembered, "Shit, I got to go! Bye! Jace!"

I heard laughter behind me "Bye Hayley, be careful." I ran down the hallway up the stairs to Mr. Night's room. "I'm here!" I said as I walked through the door.

"Well no duh. Be quiet, you are so loud! Did you get me lunch?" he asked from his desk.

"No was I supposed to?"

"Yes, but I'll just eat yours." He said walking up and grabbed my pizza from my hand and ate it in two bites.

"What-did you- what? WHY?" I screamed.

He just laughed and petted me on my head. "You are so cute when you get mad." He said smiling down at me. I frowned and scrunched up my nose. He was so mean. "Don't worry you can have these," he said while walking to his desk and pulling out a huge back of cheese puffs. I smiled and grabbed them from his hand, ripped open the bag and began devouring them. I loved these.   "Thanks!"

"No problem," he said softly and watched me with his intense blue eyes. I felt my stomach start to fill with butterflies, I was suddenly nervous, I couldn't look at him.

I head soft laughter as I looked up he was right in front of me, "Hayley," he said sweetly, I could feel his breath on my skin, I dropped the bag of cheese puffs while I shivered, felling strange and uneasy, but happy. "I'm going to do something you or the school board isn't going to like," he said backing me into the door and locking it.

"What-"then I was cut off by Logan's soft lips on mine. It was a sweet kiss, tender and loving, but quickly turned into a passionate lust filled one. He kissed me hard and I kissed him back. I threw my arms around his neck, while he grabbed my legs and brought them around his waist. He walked over to the desk and set me on it. Licking my bottom lip asking for entrance, something I gladly gave to him. We continued to make out for what seemed like hours, but when the end bell rang I jumped and drew away from him, looking into his eyes, in horror of what he and I just did. "Hayley," he said sweetly, "I don't regret it." then he kissed me again lightly on the lips and walked out of the room, leaving me there shocked and nervous.

He said he didn't regret it. Does that mean he likes me? Wait why I would care. Just an hour ago I said I hated him that I couldn't stand him. But did I really hate him? Maybe I in some ways liked him? Did I like my bio teacher? SHIT! I'm in love with my bio teacher. But before I had time to think about consequences or anything a musical voice cut me from my thoughts.

"Well wasn't that just sweet? Well now I get to see what Logan was talking about. For all his gloating about you, you aren't really much to look at aren't you? You are rather plan, borderline ugly, you also look like a four year old. Hahaha! I have nothing to worry about. Logan will be mine soon enough with a little girl like you." I looked up at the person was bashing me left and right. My mouth dropped open. She was beautiful, she had big brown eyes, long brown hair, she dressed sexily and yet it wasn't slutty it was sophisticated. She was the most beautiful girl I've ever seen.

"Who are you?"

"I'm Jasmine, Logan's girlfriend."

Chapter 8: Jasmine, The Bitch and The Werewolf

Hayley's POV:

"You're what?" I asked my voice shaking. What does she mean? I mean I know what she means but, he just kissed me and said he didn't regret it. Damn it! I am so confused.

"You heard me midget! I'm Logan's girl friend! So stay away from him. He's mine! Even if you tried you couldn't steal him from me! You aren't even a threat to me. Like come on look at you! You are like what? Five foot at best. You have limp, oily hair, your skin is dry, and you are as pale as snow. You can't even see half of your face with those hideous glasses! Plus look at the way you dress! Don't get me started! And to top of that you are a child! You could never temp Logan in the way I could. You are no more than a little fan girl trying to get the attention of super star. Give up."

That's it. This bitch is going down. "Okay seriously? If I'm not a threat why are you so worried? If I really wasn't a threat like you claim you wouldn't even be bothered to be here. You better check you're so called hold of him. Just yesterday he said he was single. Watch it, you aren't nothing but a Barbie doll prissy bitch."

"Watch it human." She warned, her features changing, she almost looked predatory.

"Human? Aren't you one two? Running out of come backs? You are nothing but a wannabe."

"What did you just call me?" she said, she looked pretty scary to me.

"You heard me bitch. You want to fight, bring it hoe."

"You do not want to provoke me. Trust me." She said her eyes looking murderous. Her lips pealed back into a growl, what the hell? Was she some sort of dog? She sure looked like one with her long carnivorous teeth. Wait! Her teeth, shit! What was wrong with this girl? Her whole body started to shake, what was going on?

"Jasmine!" a voice from behind shouted. "No!" I turned it was Logan.

"Ahhh!" I turned and suddenly there was a huge wolf in front of me. It looked like it was going to attack me.

"Jasmine, stay still do not move." Logan commanded.

"What the hell." I said completely shocked. "What the hell? WHAT THE FREAKING HELL? That's Jasmine! What the hell is going on?"

"Hayley, please leave the room. I'll talk to you later." Logan said.

"Logan what the hell is going on?" I asked.

"Just leave don't tell anyone. I'll explain later. I promise."

"When?" I asked still looking at the huge wolf that seemed to want to kill me.

"After school, normal detention time, just go now."

I nodded and walked out the door, slamming it shut. WHAT THE HELL JUST HAPPENED? Then I ran for my life to the girl's bathroom and stayed in there till school was over. I kept trying to forget what just happened. Or maybe I was dreaming? I kept trying to think of way that made what just happened in the bio room possible. And I had nothing by the time the end bell rang.

Logan's POV:

I walked out of the class room trying to explode of happiness. I kissed her. I kissed my mate. It was the most amazing kiss I have ever had. I was half way down the hall when I thought why the hell was I walking away I should have been with her. She must be confused and embarrassed and I left her alone. I sighed and mentally slapped myself and started to walk back. "What did you just call me?" what the heck? It sounded like Jasmine.

"You heard me bitch. You want to fight, bring it hoe." Hayley? Shit, Jasmine that bitch. I was going to rip her into shreds if she even touched my mate. I ran to the class room in time to hear Jasmine shout "You do not want to provoke me. Trust me." Crap I knew what was coming next. I watched in horror as Jasmine started to shift in front of Hayley. I had to stop this.

"Jasmine!" I called walking into the room. "No!" I was too late. She shifted. Thankfully Hayley didn't see the transformation. She was looking at me, her eyes wide open from fear. "Jasmine, stay still do not move." I commanded using the full force of my dominance to keep her still.

"What the hell. What the hell? WHAT THE FREAKING HELL? That's Jasmine! What the hell is going on?"Hayley shouted it looked as if she was going to have a panic attack. My poor angel.

"Hayley, please leave the room. I'll talk to you later." I said trying to reassure her.

"Logan what the hell is going on?" I smiled slightly at her use of my name, forgetting for just a moment the situation I was in.

"Just leave don't tell anyone. I'll explain later. I promise."

"When?" she asked looking nervously at Jasmine, like she afraid that she was going to hurt her. But Hayley had nothing to worry about. If Jasmine even moved a step I would rip her into pieces.

"After school, normal detention time, just go now." I said.

She nodded and ran out the door. I turned to Jasmine who was now in her human form, down on her knee, bowing her head down in respect. I just glared at her; even though she was looking down I know she could feel the intensity of my stare. "Jasmine," I said sweetly, "What were you doing here?"

She flinched at the sound of my voice. "I was going waiting to talk to you but-"

"I DON'T CARE!" I screamed. "I COMMANDED YOU TO STAY AWAY AND YOU DIDN'T LISTEN!"

"I'm sorry." She said.

"SORRY ISN'T ENOUGH!"

"Well she is human! If I don't kill her don't you think someone else would have? I'm not the only one upset about this! If it wasn't for your father and the fact no one knows what she looks like people would have already tried to kill her."

I was shaking with anger, I wanted to kill her, but I couldn't. Not now. School was still in session and students will start coming in soon. "Leave, go home. We will talk about this later." She waited for a moment thinking about something. "LEAVE NOW! AND DON'T YOU DARE GO NEAR HAYLEY OR I WILL RIP OUT YOUR THROAT."

She flinched and frowned. "Thank you." She said thinking that I let her off easy, well she had something coming to her cause no way was I going to let her get away with threatening my mate.

"Don't thank me yet, I'm not done with you yet." I said with the threat of death in my voice. She just walked away in a hurry, and I sighed and frowned. Now I'm going to have to tell Hayley the truth. I went through the rest of my classes on auto pilot frustrated and annoyed. The final bell rang and I sat at my desk waiting for my angel to walk into the room.

Chapter 9: Part One, You're a What?

C hapter 9

Hayley's pov:

I hesitated as I stood out of room 666, I was procrastinating. I in no way wanted to believe what I seen was reality. I couldn't have been more scared in my life at that moment. Today had been the most confusing day I have ever lived. First Mr. Night kisses me. Then his crazy girlfriend starts a fight with me all ending with a huge wolf standing in front of my looking like it wanted to jump and kill me.

I don't think I can take the truth, I just wanted to wake up from this nightmare and pretend this never happened. I turned around and started to run. I ran down the hallways and out the door. I ran into town just looking for something to do to get my mind off what I think would be considered the impossible. Let me just tell you one thing, Carter Town is a small boring town. I just walked through the streets for about two hours just trying to get my head straight. By the time I got to Luke's, (Gilmore Girls is the best TV show ever.) a small coffee shop that served not only the best coffee but also the best food in the world, honestly, I wanted to marry the cook, I only knew a few things that were a fact. One: That my bio teacher kissed me. Two: His girlfriend did not like me. Three: I saw a wolf in the bio room. Four: A huge wolf seemed to have been Logan's psycho girlfriend. And Five: I think I liked my bio teacher. And I have no idea which one was worse. I walked into Luke's and grabbed a table by the window waiting for the waiter. I just sat there and looked out the window trying to think of how I was going to explain what I had seen, and believe it really happened.

I also thought of what Mr. Night's expression was going to be in school next Monday since I ditched him after school today. But how could he blame me? I just sat there letting everything sink in, maybe it was all a dream? But before I could continue my thought process I heard a voice drag me from my thoughts. "Hey, what can I get you?" I looked up and it was Jace. He looked at me his eyes lighting up in recognition and said, "Oh! Hey Hayley! How are you?"

I smiled at him sweetly, "I'm good, you know, it's been crazy and all. My teacher kissed me, and I think his girlfriend is really a wolf, you know all that jazz." Well that's what I wanted to say, but I don't really want to admit I was crazy, so I settled for "I'm good, you know, it's only been like four hour since I've seen you so not much has changed." Correction, everything has changed, I thought.

He laughed and said "So what can I get you?"

"I'm going to have three cheeseburgers with a 3 large side of fries, a chicken salad two chili fries and two litters of coke, to go please."

He looked at me funny for a minute then wrote down my order, nodded and left. Ten minutes later he was back with a huge brown bag and the check. "Are you planning on eating that all by yourself?" He asked as I handed him the money.

"Are you serious? Of course not! Half of it's for my uncle." He laughed and waved goodbye as I walked out the door. I walked to the police station said hi to Larry one of the cops and went to my uncles desk. "David!" I called. Looking as my uncle whose face was buried in piles and piles of papers.

He looked up in shock and smiled when he saw me. "HAYYY-LEYYY! YAY! YOU CAME TO SEE ME!" he said getting up and hugging me tightly.

I could barely breathe when I choke out "Can't breath-"he looked at me with a panicked expression and patted my back. When I could finally breathe I put his half of the food, a cheeseburger, the chicken salad, a side of fried and a litter of coke on the desk. "Since you said you'll be working a case till tomorrow I brought you food so you could work straight on your case till you're done. You're going to Rochester tonight right? Just eat this and go straight there so you can get home faster."

He looked at me, his eyes started to well up as he gave me another big hug "Hayley! You care about me! Oh I love you! You are the perfect daughter." He cooed. God I hated it when he said that. I just nodded struggled out of his grasp and said "Okay I got to go. See you on Sunday uncle." I walked out as fast as I could with the rest of my food.

"It's DADDY!" he called. I just sighed and went home.

I walked through the town to Markus Street and got to my house. I opened the door and set the food down so I could close the front door and locked it. I went to the kitchen and put my food down on the table and got out a few plates. I put my food on the plates and microwave it. I sat at the table as I waited and thought about everything that happened today. I shook my head and decided it was my overactive imagination playing tricks on me and it never happened.

Yes, I said to myself, it was you your imagination. I almost screamed in frustration as I pulled my food out of the microwave and ran to my room. As I opened the door I saw sitting on my bed looking at me with disapproving eyes, the last person I ever wanted to see. But how was that possible? I rubbed my eyes, hoping that I was just imaging things, but sadly when I heard his low husky voice I knew for a fact I wasn't just losing my mind. "So Hayley, you didn't come to see me. I was quiet upset you know."

I almost dropped my food as I started to curse, I said every bad word I knew trying to think of some explanation of how in god's name did my hot bio teacher get in my bed room. "What? How the hell?"

He looked at me exasperated and said "Well I waited for you for an hour after school and when you never came I came here. I've been waiting in your small room for hours, just so I could talk to you about what happened today."

It really happened, I thought. After all this, after all the convincing I went through today to believe that everything I saw was just me losing it, it was all real. I set my food down on my desk and sat down next to Logan in defeat. "It was all real?" I asked, more to myself then him.

"Yep." He said and pulled his arms around me enveloping me in a hug.

"What happened?" I asked looking into his beautiful blue eyes. We just stared at each other for a long time, when finally he took his hands and placed them on either side of my face, and brought his lips to mine. At first I struggled, hitting him and trying to escape his grasp but soon I gave up and began kissing him back. As I wrapped my arms around his neck, and his hands were at my waist I wondered how this happened. All I wanted to know was the truth and this is how we end up. But no matter how much my common sense told me to stop I just couldn't. I needed him; I needed to feel his touch I needed his lips on mine. As the kisses got deeper, he shifted so I was under him and he was on top of me, hovering over me so I wasn't crushed beneath his weight. Even though he was trying not to crush me I needed to feel his body against mine, I brought my arms around his shoulders trying to get closer to him as I wrapped my legs around his waist. He moaned in my mouth. My hormones went crazy as I felt him 'raise' against my thigh, it felt really good. "Hayley." He growled.

I smiled at his response; I pulled away from him kissing his neck slowly, sucking on different parts, trying to find his soft spot. When I found it he moaned and said "Stop teasing me." I smirked against his neck, I continued to kiss him, his ear lobe, his neck, his jaw, his check, he seemed to be sick of this as he brought my lips back up to his. We continued to kiss, I brought my hands under his shirt feeling his nice toned abs softly brushing my hands against his stomach. He shivered under my touch and growled, kissing my neck biting me.

Wait my head said, he growled. I sat up with a shock. Wolves, was all I could think of. "Hayley?" Logan asked his voice careful.

"What happened? In the bio room? One minute Jamie was there and the next there was a wolf. And wait a minute! Jamie said she was your girlfriend. What's going on? I'm so confused. Logan what the hell is going on?"

He looked at me for a minute, like he was debating something. "Hayley, come with me." He said getting up off the bed holding his hand out for me to hold it.

"What-"

"Shut up for just a minute. Come with me and I'll explain everything." He said tenderly. I just nodded silently and grabbed his hand. He guided me through my house and waited for me to put on my shoes. When I noticed he wasn't wearing any he just shook his head and lead me outside to the wood. I looked up at the sky, it was nighttime so soon. The moon was out. "So, first of all," he started as we walked through the trees. "Her name is Jasmine." My heart felt a pang of jealously and sadness. "Secondly, she isn't my girlfriend. She is far from it." I nodded somehow feeling much better at that little piece of knowledge. He didn't say anything for awhile as we continued to walk through the woods, finally stopping in a meadow, far from the path. "Also," he finally said stopping. "Jasmine is a werewolf." I just looked at him in awe. Sure I just wanted to laugh it off as a joke but I really couldn't. I couldn't deny what I had seen with my own eyes, no matter how much I really wanted to. "And so am I." I just looked at him, unable to say anything. "Hayley," he started, taking off his shirt.

I gasped, what is he doing? "What are you doing?! Don't take your clothes off!" I was blushing furiously. He smiled and laughed at my embarrassment.

"Don't look then." But I was unable to once I saw his glorious body under the moonlight. I watched him as he took of the rest of his clothes. He was beautiful. And even though what he had just told me scared the hell out of me I couldn't deny my overwhelming feelings towards him, even though they were unexplainable. I watched his naked body start to shake, his beautiful blue eyes seemed to glow in the moon light, they never leaved my face as I saw his body shift slowly, looking more and more like a canine then human. I watched at his spine seemed to arch, his body get hairy, his teeth growing into scarp razors, able to rip human flesh and bones without even a difficulty. His hands clawed up, his fingers turning into paws, I gaped at him as he became one of the most beautiful creatures I have ever seen.

I looked at the beautiful wolf in front of me. He was the same one I saw just this morning on my way to school. He was midnight black, he was huge, nothing about this glorious creature looked like the man I called my bio teacher, nothing besides his lovely eyes that I have grown so found of. "Logan?" I asked. The wolf seemed too smiled at me in confirmation. I walked towards him slowly, cautious, as though I was afraid it would run, even though deep down I knew he never would run from me. As I walked closer Logan looked at me through his big eyes filled with love and awe. I was next to him, as I petted his head softly "You're beautiful." I said. He seemed to laugh as he sat down, I laid down next to him, cuddling up in his soft fur. "Even though I think I should be afraid of you, I'm not. Is that weird?" I asked.

The wolf just looked at me and rolled its eyes. "You know I never thought this would happen? Just yesterday we met. And just this morning I hated you. How did this happen? It seems like I've known you forever." I was shocked at how much I was saying but for some reason it felt comfortable about how much I was sharing with him. Logan didn't say anything, he couldn't. I just lay against him, loving the fell of his warmth. I was staring at the sky looking at the stars and moon, as I slowly drifted into a deep sleep.

"UGH" I said, rolling over in bed. I didn't want to get up, I was so warm and comfortable, so I rolled over again and hit something. It felt like a hard rock. I pried my eyes open and saw Logan. What was he doing in my bed? And why were his arms around me? Memories from yesterday came back to me in flash of confusion. I looked around me, I wasn't in my bed. I had no freaking idea where I was. I looked around me, I was in a white room, that was as big as my whole bottom floor of my house. Okay maybe not that big but it was huge. I looked back at Logan and realized something. He was naked. "AHHHHHH" I scream. He stirred in his sleep holding me tighter to him. "OH MY GOD! LOGAN! GET OFF OF ME. WHY THE HELL AREN'T YOU WEARING ANY CLOTHES? LOGAN?"

He seemed to finally get the hint and wake up. He looked at me in annoyance. "Hayley, please be a little quieter in the morning. I'm tired."

"You're tired? Are you kidding me? First of all I have no idea where I am. Second of all you are some freaky type of werewolf. And thirdly you're naked."

He looked at me and sighed. "You are in my apartment. I am a werewolf, a fact you seemed to have taken in quiet well." He looked at my panicked face and shook his head. "Well yesterday you took it well. And yea so what if I'm naked. I had to carry you on my back so when I got here I didn't feel like changing. So I put you on the bed and fell asleep next to you."

I looked at him in horror. "Put some clothes on!" he sighed and started to get up. "Wait!"

"What?" he said, he was definitely annoyed with me now.

I pulled the covers over my head and said "Okay, get up now, and tell me when I can look."

I heard his musical laughter. After about a minute I heard him say "Okay."

I pulled the over off of me and found myself face to face with Logan, his blue eyes smothering me with sweetness. "AHH!" I said pulling the covers over my face again.   "What now?"

"Don't look at me like that!"

"Why not?"

"Because I said so."

He laughed again and pulled the covers back off my face and kissed me. I was in shock at first then I kissed him back.

Chapter 9: Part Two, You're a What?

Okayyy, heres chapter 9...part two...sorry it's late.

vote and comment please?

Chapter 9

Hayley's POV:

It took about 30 minutes to finally get Logan off me, and kick him out of the room (his room lol) just to get my head around everything that had happened. He was a werewolf, my teacher, and possibly my boyfriend. I wonder what my mom is thinking of all this while looking down at me from heaven, she is probably shaking her head laughing right now at my confusion. How did I get myself into this mess?

I got up slowly and realized I was only in my underwear and a t-shirt, one I was sure was not mine, just considering the fact it went just above my knee. My face heated up realizing that Logan must have changed my clothes last night.

"LOGAN NIGHT I'M GOING TO KICK YOU'RE ASS!" I screamed running out of the bedroom. "SERIOUSLY YOU COULDN'T HAVE JUST-" I stopped screaming when I saw a shirtless Logan hugging a small red head. My first reaction was rage. HE WAS MINE, no way was I going to let anyone take him from me. Then all I felt was sadness and misery. Logan, who must have felt my presence looked up at me in shock. "Okay, I'll just leave now." I said running past both of them, tears in my eyes, out of the apartment and down the hall.

"Hayley, wait-" I heard Logan say, I just kept running down the stairs outside to the street. Shit, I thought as my feet hit the pavement, it was like 5:00am and it was cold and I only had a t-shirt on, I didn't even have my shoes. "Hayley Lake stop right there!" I heard Logan call from behind me.

I wanted to run, but I also wanted to hear what he said. After a moment of internal debate I sighed and turned around. "WHY? I mean why am I here, with you? You are all over me one minute then hugging some other girl while I'm in the same room. Please stop giving me mixed signals, I am confused enough already."

He smiled at me, I momentarily forgot I was mad at him as I stared into his blue eyes, "Hayley, that was my old friend Macy, he mate-her boy friend and her just had a huge fight and she was really upset. So she came here to talk to me, she really needed a friend. Trust me, Macy and I, well it would never happen."

I felt like the biggest jerk in the whole wide world when he said that. Her boyfriend and her just had a huge fight and then I had to go and bitch, ugh. "Oh god Logan, I'm sorry I was horrible I was just so confused I guess...I have no idea what's been getting into me lately." I said walking up to him slowly and giving him a hug.

His face lit up like a child on Christmas Eve when I wrapped my arms around him. He brought his large arms around my body and took hold of my waist with his hands. "I do!" he said cheerfully. "You're jealous!"

I just stared at him in horror, I was not jealous. "I am not jealous." I denied.

"Sure you aren't sweetheart."

"I'm not!" I insisted.

"Okay, keep convincing yourself that, but in the mean time can we go inside it's freezing and no matter how hot you look, I bet even you are getting a little cold." I looked at him questioning his meaning, then I looked down and remembered what I was wearing. I blushed and tried to pull the t-shirt down a little but to no avail it would not get any long. He just smirked at me and smacked my barely covered ass. "HEY!" I shouted. He smiled and led me back up to his apartment. "You were jealous." He chanted.

"Was not."

"Was to."

"Was not."

"Was to."

"Was not."

"Was to."

"No."

"Yes."

"No."

"Yes."

"NO I WASN'T."

"Yes you were, now shut up for a minute and let me enjoy this," he said, I could hear the smile in his voice. As we reached his door I was about to smack him when I saw the little redhead was still there.

"Hello," she said timidly. "I'm sorry, what you saw wasn't what you thought-"

I cut her off before she could continue. "No I'm sorry. I was overreacting."

"You weren't you are his mate after all."

"Huh?" I asked confused. What as a mate? Wasn't that British for friend? She looked at me in wonder then up at Logan behind me. Her face looked shocked then she rearranged her features into a smile. "So Hayley, Logan said you had glasses. Where are they?"

CRAP! I just noticed I wasn't wearing them. I ran to the bedroom and checked all over for them, they weren't there. "Logan! Have you seen my glasses?" I asked as I walked back into the main room.

"Yea, I broke them in two. You don't need them and you look better without them." He said matter of factly. Macy just looked at him like she expected him to say something like that. But I was pissed as hell.

"What do you mean? Logan! I needed those!"

"No you didn't."

"Yes I did."

"Okay, no you didn't now shut it before I decide not to make you breakfast." I shut up quickly realizing how hungry I was. I nodded and sat down at the counter in the kitchen next to where Macy was sitting.

"So Hayley, how old are you?" Macy asked as Logan started to make pancakes, sausage and eggs.

"I'm 16 turning 17 soon."

"Oh really? When's your birthday?"

"April 6th."

"Oh so you're a junior?"

"Yep." I answered, marveling at her beauty, it was almost unfair how pretty she was. She wasn't in your face pretty but she was quiet cute, I was jealous.

"Oh."

"So how old are you?"

"I'm 20, a year younger then Logan." I gaped at her, she looked even younger than me, how was that possible. "Yea I look young for my age."

I smiled at her. Then I thought of something, if Logan was a were-wolf, could it be possible that Macy was too? "Umm so are you a...I mean are you...like Logan? What I mean is are you a-"

"Yes I'm a werewolf." She said

"Oh..."

"Yup! So are you going to dinner tonight?" She asked her eyes lit up in excitement. What dinner? CRASH! I looked up, Logan had dropped a plate and it was now smashed into millions of little pieces. "Idiot." Macy mumbled.

"Macy, I think you should leave now."

"Awww, Logan! Don't be mad at me! She should meet the pack sooner or later." Pack? As in pack of werewolves?

"Macy, leave. I'll see you tonight." Logan said threatening. Damn he looked scary.

"Fine, but you should tell her. And I'm not scared of you. If you want to rip my throat out, just try." She said staring at him with a menacing look and walked out. I just stared after her in awe, who would have thought that little thing could stick up to Logan, I mean he was huge and definitely scary. "Here" Logan said setting a plate of food in front of my face.

I smiled up at him happily, "Thanks!" And I dug in, I was starving. I just ate as Logan watched my laughing in amusement across me leaning against the counter. "So," I started to say but was soon cut off by Logan's sexy voice. "Chew first, talk second."

I sighed and finished my bite of pancake, which by the way it was the best pancake I have ever eaten. It was just awesome. "What did she mean by pack? Like of werewolves, do I get to meet them tonight?" I said excitedly. Now that the idea of werewolves fully sunk in I was quiet happy with the idea.

"I am going to kill Macy!" He huffed.

I smiled and put a hand on hand on his cheek and gave him a quick kiss, "Don't be, I liked her. She was funny, and she stood up to you, you need a little ego burst once in awhile."

He just smiled at me and said "Trust me sweetheart, you're my daily ego burst." I just smiled and continued eating, "And yes a pack means werewolves, a lot of them. Aren't you scared of that idea at all?"

I looked at him in shock, "If I had been scared why would I still be here? I mean I love wolves why wouldn't I love the idea of were-wolves?"

"You sure are something." He said looking at me with an unreadable expression.

"So do I get to meet them? Is it a big dinner tonight? Like the whole pack or just important people? Do I get to meet the, ummm what do they call it? Alpha, yea I think that's it. Do I get to meet the Alpha?"

He looked at me apprehensively and nodded, "It's a family dinner, it my mother my father, my best friend, and a few other close members of the pack."

"Oh okay. So can I go? Or would that be inappropriate? Since I have no idea what I am to you..." I said fading off. Shit, I said something I really shouldn't have. God, this is what I get for talking, I never talk. I liked it that way, and now that I finally feel comfortable with him I've become a babbling idiot. Crap.

He laughed at me and kissed my cheek, "You mean everything to me, and don't doubt it okay? You can come at your own risk. My family is quiet...odd. I really would rather you not, just because they are werewolves and you...aren't, but if you really want..."

That was right, I wasn't a werewolf...he probably has someone else, someone of his...species. I was just a human, he could never actually care about me. He seemed to sense my uncertainty when he brought his lips to mine, kissing my sweetly and softly. "You are my only one. I really care for you." He said drawing away from me, but only a little our noses touching, I could feel his sweet breath against my skin.

I smiled at him sadly. "But I'm human-"

"Shut up. I don't care."

"I'm your student."

"I still don't care."

"We can't have an open relationship."

"So?"

"We can't hold hands or go places together in public."

"I don't care. It's better that way, I don't have to share you."

"I met you two days ago."

He just laughed, "Honey, it doesn't matter. Whether we've known each other forever or an hour, we still have the same chance of lasting as everyone."

I just smiled at him, he kissed me again and drew away. "Thanks." I said.

"You're welcome, girlfriend." I smiled at the sound of it. Then he pulled away and started to clean up the kitchen. I continued to eat, when I was done I brought my plate to him and said, "Can I take a shower?"

"Yea, it's the door to the left." I nodded and walked towards the door, "You know," he called from behind me. "I could always join you."

"You pervert!" I screamed, blushed and ran into the bathroom. I looked at the mirror my face was beat red, ugh I hated what he did to me, but it made me really happy at the same time. I stripped down and walked into the shower, loving the feeling of the warm water run down my body. When I got out and wrapped the towel around me I realized I had no clothes. Shit I would have to go out there in a towel, or I could just... "Logan?" I said sticking my head out of the door way.

"Yea."

"Where are my clothes?"

"In the room."

"Can you grab them for me?" I asked sweetly.

"Sure-wait a minute. You didn't bring your clothes in there?"

"Nope..."

"Go and get them yourself."

"What? No why?"

"So I can see you in that little towel thats why."

"Logan please!" I begged.

"Nope."

"You suck."

"That's your job." My face was now the color of a tomato.

"Fuck you."

"Please?" he asked. God I really wanted to hit him, I took a deep breath and ran to the bedroom, and very aware of the fact the towel barely covered my ass. I got to the bedroom and closed the door quickly. I put my clothes on from last night and then walked back out of the room, ready to face the devil. I walked to the living room, walking in front of the tv Logan was watching my hands on my hips, I went up to him grabbed a pillow and wacked him on the head. "Yes darling?" he said innocently.

"I hate you."

"No you don't."

"Do too." Then he smiled wickedly and grabbed the pillow next to him and hit me on the head. I looked at him shocked then wacked him again. Soon it was a full blown pillow fight. We just kept hitting each other, laughing at the others face. We continued this for awhile till he ended on top of my hitting me softly on the head. "I win!" He announced.

"No way."

"Yup! I WON!" he screamed then kissed me. It was first a light kiss, but soon got heated and more passionate. I threw my hands around his neck as he kissed my neck, I moaned with pleasure as he sucked on the sensitive part at the base of my collar bone. I sighed in happiness and just happened to see the clock, it was 12:20. Crap. I shot up startling Logan. "Take me home."

He looked hurt, and I felt bad immediately. "No why?"

"I need to get something nice to wear."

"Why?" he asked in confusion.

"Dinner."

He sighed a sigh of relief, then quickly looked annoyed. "Oh yea, it doesn't matter what you wear. You'll look beautiful no matter what."

"I don't care. When is dinner?"

He looked at me hesitantly, like he didn't want to answer my question. "I should be there at 4:00."

I nodded, "Just take me home." He sighed got up took my hand and lead me out the door.

When we got to my house, I walked up to the front door opened it ran upstairs Logan at my heels. "Okay, what should I wear?" I asked him looking at my closet unable to find anything suitable, I mean all I owned were jeans.

"I don't care." He said looking around my room.

"You are useless." I said and grabbed a mid thigh jean skirt Jane left here last time she was over. I went into the bathroom and changed into it and a pink tank top. I looked in the mirror frowning, I looked awful. "Okay, tell me how bad." I said and walked back into my room. Logan looked up at me from my bed, his eyes glazing over with lust.

"You look good." He said dryly, staring at my legs.

I smirked and said, "We should go. It's like 2:30. How far away does your family live?"

He was still staring when he said "30 minutes away, Elizabeth town."

Elizabeth Town? My grandma lives there. "Really! My grandmother lives there." I said excitedly.

He just smiled and said "Really? Cool."

"Yep, but we should go! Come on." I said dragging him out of my house and back to his car.

"Are you sure about this?" he asked as we stood out of his house. I just stared at his house, which was about the size of a mansion, I mean seriously? How many people lived in there? I just nodded unable to speak. "Okay, let's go in then." He grabbed my hand and lead me to the front door. I felt so small as he knocked on the door. When the door opened a beautiful woman was standing there smiling. "LOGAN! SWEETIE! I'M SO GLAD YOU DECIDED TO COME! When Macy said you might be I got so excited. I made your favorite. Beef stew!"

Logan stood there smiling at the women. I realized they had the same eyes. "Mom, chill. This is Hayley," he said gesturing to me at his side. The women looked at me with shock at first then a smile.

"Hayley!" She said giving me a huge hug. "You mean she's your ma-"

"She's my girl friend." Logan said cutting her off.

"Oh, you mean she doesn't know?"

"I know you're werewolves." I said. Logan's mom just looked at him and he nodded. Okay...?

"Okay, that's good. One step at a time." she said more to herself than anyone else. "Anyways I'm Debra Night."(I don't remember if I had already given her a name...)

I smiled and said "Nice to meet you Mrs. Night."

"Oh honey, please call me Debra or mom, anything. Mrs. Night makes me feel old, like my mother in law." She said leading us in the house, it was even bigger on the inside then it was on the outside.

I laughed. "That's what Logan said about his dad."

"Oh really" Came a deep voice, I looked up and it was a good looking man in his late 30 early 40s, it was like staring at the future Logan. "Logan my boy, do I really look that old to you?"

Logan just laughed and said "To me dad you are. This is Hayley, my girlfriend."

His dad looked at me and smiled. "Nice too meet you Hayley."

"You too Mr. Night."

"Call me Cam." He said warmly.

"Okay."

"Wow, Logan, you really brought that human to dinner? I'm shocked you had the guts." said a familiar voice. I looked up it was Jasmine, oh great. This night was going to suck.

Chapter 10: Dinner With The Nights

Chapter 10: Dinner With The Nights

Hayley's POV:

So the atmosphere was awkward and stressed. Logan kept looking at me, Jasmine was glaring at me, and Mr. and Mrs. Night just smiled at me. "So Hayley, are you okay with all this werewolf stuff?" Mr. Night asked as we stood in the living room.

"Umm, yea," I answered. "I've always had a thing for wolves, so my boyfriend being one doesn't bug me. Well not as much as him being my teacher, that tends to bug me." I said, surprised at how much I was talking. Why was I talking so much? I never did. This is all getting to weird. First my teacher actually likes me. Then he becomes my boyfriend who turns out to be a werewolf. And now I was talking, could my life get any weirder?

Everyone just looked at me like I was stupid. Which I was, I mean how many girls worried more about their boyfriends being their teacher then him being a werewolf. Maybe I was losing it? It was awkward for a moment, and then I felt Logan start shaking next to me. I looked up at him in wonder. He was covering his mouth with his hand, his body just quivering. "Logan, are you okay?" his father asked looking at his son with worry.

I started to pat him on the back. "You okay?" I asked.

Then it started.

He started to laugh.

At me.

"HAHAHAHAHAHAHAHAHAAHAHAHAHAHAHA!" He laughed, bursting out so suddenly it shocked all of us. His mother and father looked at him questioning his odd behavior. Jasmine just looked at him like he was a goner. "HAHAHAHAHAHAHA-

HAHAHAHAHAHA!" he continued. He was laughing so hard he was doubling over in pain. "That was-oh my god- hahahahahahaha."

"What? Logan! Please stop laughing at me." I yelled, looking at him in panic balling up my fist.

"I'm sorry," he choked out, but he was still laughing so he had to stop, "It's just you are so cute! You worry about this weirdest thing."

"What-? Logan! You're mean!" I said hitting him lightly.

"I'm sorry sweetie, as I said you're just too cute." He said kissing me on the forehead. I blushed looking around me in embarrassment. Jasmine was throwing daggers with her eyes. And even though Mr. and Mrs. Night were smiling, I could tell it was forced. The look on their face was worry, and even slight annoyance.

"AWWWW! Now ain't that cute?" drawled a sweet voice from behind me. I turned around and saw Macy. I smiled at her. "I'm so glad you came!" Macy said, skipping up to hug me.

I was shocked at first but I just smiled and lightly hugged her back. "Yea, much to Logan's annoyance." I said looking at Logan who then stuck his tongue out at me.

"Oh don't worry about, he's just worried someone's going to slip up." She said turning around to face Logan with a smirk on her face.

Logan just glared at her, if looks could kill she'd be ten feet under, but same could have been said for me, Jasmine was still giving me the death glare. And it was making me uncomfortable. "Never mind him." Macy said, "Cam! Debra! Everyone's here." Macy said to Mr. and Mrs. Night who were watching us with their mouth open.

They seemed to shake off whatever they were thinking, and I literally mean shake, and then smiled warmly at Macy. "Oh good," Mrs. Night said happily, and she left the room, with Mr. Night and Macy at toe. Jasmines slower then both of them stalk out the room, muttering something under her breath. I looked at Logan who just looked angry.

"So," I said trying to break the awkwardness, "Do I get to meet the rest of the pack?"

He looked at me like I was crazy and said "Only a few."

"Who?" I asked excited.

He just looked at me, his face softened and said "You'll see." And took me hand and led me to the dining room. Everyone, but the Night's was already sitting down. There were three older couples, and other than Jasmine and Macy there was only one other man who I would say was Logan's age. "Hello everyone," Logan said smiling politely at them, pulling out a seat for me to sit down. And once I was seated, he sat down himself. "This is my girlfriend Hayley Lake, Hayley this is Rob and Carolyn Robin, Macy's parents." They smiled warmly at me. I smiled back. They seemed very nice, Mr. Robin had the same hair color as Macy, while Macy got her height from her mother who was rather short.

"Macy did tell us you were a very pretty girl!" Mrs. Robin said, Mr. Robin just nodded his head in agreement.

"Nice to meet you." I said a little nervously.

"Mr. Robin is what you would call omega, third in command." Logan said smiling at him fondly, "He's one hell of a fighter."

"Well, since your dad is no good at it, someone had to be." The old man said.

Logan laughed and then pointed to the next couple. The man looked very nice, while the woman, blonde hair, tall and strikingly beautiful looked at me with distain. "This is Ramon and Julia Mars, you know

Jasmine, their daughter." Logan said stiffly, "and that next to her, that ugly son of a gun is Craig, their son." He said pointing to the good looking boy who was smiling brightly at me. He had the same brown eyes as his mother and the dame dirty blond hair from his father.

"Nice to meet you Hayley, when you get sick of this old man there," Craig said pointing at Logan, "I'll be here." He said with a wink.

"Don't even try man." Logan said in annoyance.

"Hey she's cute, you can't help but try."Logan just shook his head in annoyance. "Hey don't let his attitude fool you, I'm the best friend he's got." Craig said with a smirk.

"Yea one I could do without." Logan said and laughed. "Anyways Hayley Ramon is the beta, he's the smart one, he's got all the brains."

"Yup, your father may be a good leader but he is pretty much as smart as a brick." Mr. Mars said with laughter in his voice.

"I heard that." Mr. Night said walking in and sitting down.

"You were meant to." Ramon said laughing. The men started to talk about the 'good old days' and I just sat there in thought till my phone buzzed. I excused myself and walked out the front door. Once outside I opened my phone and said "Hey?"

"HAYLEY LAKE! WHERE ARE YOU?" My uncle screamed from the other line.

"I'm home why?" I said lying though my teeth.

"No you are not. I just got a call from Noah saying that he and Jane came over for a sleepover and you weren't there."

Crap, "Okay I went to visit moms grave okay?" I said coming up with a believable lie. "I missed her and well..." I said hoping he was buying it, which was maybe unlikely since I've always refused to visit my mom's grave since she died.

"Oh...well okay then." He said awkwardly.

"Okay uncle I got to go." I said in a rush and hung up. I just stared at the phone for a minute feeling horrible about what I had just done. I debated calling him back and telling him the truth but how would that work out? 'So uncle David I lied before, I'm really at my boyfriend's house who by the way is my teacher, and I'm currently meeting his pack, oh didn't I tell you? He is also a werewolf.' I don't think that would go over to well. I looked at my phone again and realized I had 10 unread texts, all from either Noah or Jane. I sighed, I'd answer them later.

Feeling guilty I walked back into the house and made my way into the dining room. I realized everyone was sitting down looking at me expectedly, "Sorry to keep you waiting." I said embarrassed.

Everyone either smiled or looked at me with tolerance. "Is everything okay?" Logan asked as I sat down.

"Yea just my uncle checking in on me."

"Oh okay." he said.

Mrs. Night just smiled and said "Okay now everyone can eat." I had just noticed the food was on the table. Everyone grabbed the thing closes next to them and began to fill their plates then pass the dished to the left. There was chicken, turkey, ham, mash potatoes and gravy, with corn and beans. There was also rice and beef stew, which I noticed Logan liked the most, just by looking at the amount of it he put on his plate. There was also noodles and marinara sauce. And a lot of salad. Every time a dish was passed to me I'd take some of it, well all but the beans, salad and turkey. I noticed that all the women just had salad on their plate with maybe a little bit of ham, and then men had huge plates of food piled on their plate. Macy had quite a bit on hers but not as much as I did.

"Ew, how can you eat all that? You'll end up huge." Jasmine said.

"Hey, I like a girl who can eat." Craig said.

I could feel Logan's anger radiating off my body. "I'm sorry. I'd rather not die of starvation, but that's just me. And it seems I'm smaller then you any way so..."

All the women, besides Macy who was snickering, looked at me in either horror or amusement, amusement from Macy's mother and horror from Jasmine's and Logan's mother. All the fathers just laughed. Jasmine just looked as if she was going to kill me.

I looked at Logan with remorse on my face, I shouldn't have said that. But he just smiled and set his hand on mine and gave it a little squeeze. "It's okay."

The rest of the night went smoothly, I tried to just keep busy and talk to Macy and her mother and ignore the glares from Jasmine, her mother and Logan's. But no matter how much I tried to ignore it, I could still feel their burning intense looks.

So when dinner ended, it couldn't have been soon enough. "Logan," I said as he took showed me around his house before desert, "Who was the alpha, I didn't meet him."

"Yes you did." Logan said not looking at me.

"Who?"

"My father." He answered, still not looking at me.

"Your father is alpha, meaning you will be once he dies." I asked, shocked, sort of unable to really think of anything smarter to say.

"Yea, well not when he dies, when I either challenge him or he steps down."

"Oh." I said.

"Are you okay with that?" He asked finally looking at me, worried like I'd run off.

"Why shouldn't I be?" I asked

"You-never mind." he said. "Come on, we have to get back down there or mother will be angry.

"That's another thing."

"What?

"Why does your mother hate me?"

"She doesn't."

"Does too. She keeps looking at me as if I was some type of rodent and she is thinking of ways to get rid of me without bloodying her hands."

He laughed slightly, "That is a crappy analogy."

"Just answer me."

He sighed and said simply, "Because you are human."

I'm human. That's right. One day Logan will leave me, because I'm human. I'm just a play toy for now, I'll be used till he finds someone better. "That's right." I said looking down, tears in my eyes. "I'm just human. You'll find someone else soon right? Your mate, that's what you call them right. I'm just here till you find her right."

"Hayley, you're mistaken."

"Why did you have to bring me here?" I asked, looking up at him angrily, tears now streaming down my face.

"Hayley I already have a mate but she's-"

"No, just don't say anything." I said afraid to hear anymore. Afriad to get hurt. Afraid to know the truth. So I ran, I just ran out the door and to the street ignore Logan's calls from behind me. "Hayley."

"Logan, just let her go for now, you can-" I heard someone say to him, but I never heard the ending of it, I was now too far away. I ran still I was sure I was far enough I searched through my phone and saw an odd contact. But when I couldn't think of anyone else I dialed. "Hello?" his voiced answered

"Hey, it's Hayley, I for some reason had your number, I have no idea how it got in here but could I ask you for a favor?" I asked begging him.

"Sure?"

"Can you pick me up?"

"Yea sure, where are you?"

"I'm in Elizabeth town, in the square."

"That's far away from Cater. Lucky for you I'm only a few minutes from there though."

"Really, thanks."

"No problem be there in a minute." And he hung up. I just walked into the town and sat on the bench in the middle of the square, trying to pull myself together. I smiled when I saw his car. "Hey!" I said.

"Hey. Come on."

"Hayley! Wait." I turned and saw Logan running towards me looking panicked. I quickly jumped into the car and said "Hurry! Drive."

"Okayyyy." And he sped off. But I could still see through the review mirror, Logan's torn up face. I felt tears drip down my face.

"Are you okay?" he asked.

"Yea, I will be. Thanks Jace."

and vote and comment, i know this was bad :(sorry....

Chapter 11: I'm your what?

Logan's POV:

Was it possible that your heart hurt so bad you felt as if you were dying? Well honestly I think it's possible. Right now my heart hurts so bad I feel as though it had been ripped out of my chest then fed to wild animals.

When Hayley left me standing on the street I felt like my whole world ended. She was my life my light my lover my mate and I needed her.

I wasn't going to let her go, and neither was my wolf. Right now he was devastated and upset, but he was also determined to get what was his back. Even if she wanted me to, I wasn't going to give her up.

To anyone. Not even if she wanted to leave me I'd chase her to the end of the world.

When she got in the car with that stupid Jace kid I wanted to hunt him down and rip out this throat. I wanted to tear him limb from limb then feed the remains to a pack of rogue wolves.

I shifted into my wolf form and began to chase after her. Even though me getting her back was important her safety came first.

I would watch over her till she was alone. Then I would tell her the truth. I'd tell her she was my mate and I needed her. I'd tell her I loved her and wanted her with all my heart. I'll tell her that she is mine and I was hers.

I would get her back.

Hayley's POV:

The ride back to town was silent and awkward. Jace didn't ask any questions and for that I was glad he didn't. I just looked out the window fighting tears. Even though it had no right to, my heart was breaking into a million little pieces and there was nothing I could do about it.

Once we had reached the outskirts of town Jace finally said, "It's going to be alright. It's not the end of the world."

Even though I knew that, it felt like it was. Leaving Logan there hurt me more than it should have. I shouldn't already feel like we were just two parts of a puzzle, but I did. I felt like if he wasn't mine I would die. "Thanks, I know, it just hurts right now."

"It's going to, just try to move on." He said sympathetically. "I know how you feel when Cary broke up with me, it felt like the end of the world. But now I know it's not."

I looked at him in awe, he knew how I felt, and he got over it. How did he do that? "How? How do you get over this type of heart break?" I asked, just wanting the pain I felt in my chest to disappear.

"You meet new people I guess? You keep moving on with your life and sometimes if you're lucky, you'll meet someone who makes you forget all those feelings you once had."

"Did you?" I asked

He nodded thoughtfully for a moment and said "Yea, I did."

I didn't pry any longer, if he wanted to tell me he would. I sighed as I gave him directions to my house. Once we got there he said "I know it hurts like hell now, but you'll be okay, I have a good feeling about it." he said with a smile.

I smiled back at him and nodded. I'd be okay. "Thanks, for the ride, thanks for everything." "No problem. See you on Monday." Then he drove off. I looked at my house, not wanting to be a lone in there. But where else could I go? So I reluctantly went up stairs and took a shower. Loving the feeling of the warm water running down my back, I just sat there. I thought of Logan's face before I drove off, it was heart breaking. I just cried and cried.

Suddenly I felt a pair of strong arms wrap around me holding me comforting me. "I'm so sorry." He whispered. He turned the water off and draped a huge towel over my body, picked me up and laid me on the bed. He just held me, letting me cry, mumbling, "I'm sorry." Over and over again, even though he had nothing to be sorry about. It wasn't his fault, not in the slightest.

Once I was done crying, he left the room, leaving me to get changed. I just put on my underwear my bra a tank top and a pair of pajama shorts. The weird thing was he seemed to sense when I was done changing and walked back into the room, and hugged me. He had me in a death grip, like at any moment I would run. And believe me, the thought of him leaving me made me want to run for my life. But I just stood there his arms around me, loving the feel of my sanity back. "I don't care." I said, "I don't care if I'm human, and you would one day leave me, I don't care anymore. I need you, and I want you, and I'm going to hold onto you till the day you go, and after that I will fight for you." I said, confidently and sad at the same time. Realizing the truth in the matter, I loved him and I never wanted to be away from him.

I heard him laugh slightly, I was sort of annoyed, I just spilled my guts and how he was laughing how typical.

I looked up at Logan, looking into his beautiful blue eyes, knowing that the moment I would do that, my angry would disappear and all that I would see was him. "Hayley, you misunderstand so easily. You know that right?" I was about to protest when he said "If you wouldn't have ran out I would have told you right away and you wouldn't have cried." He said running his fingers over my cheeks, "Hayley, you are my mate." He said proudly, full of love and awe.

I just stared at him blankly. I was his mate? I bitched and cried and it ended up I was over reacting. I just stood there feeling stupid and dumb. "I'm so sorry." I said hugging him tightly, feeling tears well up in my eyes again. "I'm such a kid, I didn't mean to overreact, it just when you said I was human, suddenly reality hit me and I just...oh god! I'm so sorry Logan.

He laughed and said "It's alright, you know? You have a choice, as a human you can leave me, if you want to tell me now." He said staring into my eyes, his blue eyes were serious.

"I don't want you to leave me. Didn't we just go through this?" I said, returning his intense stare.

He smiled at me and said "I love you."

And even though I didn't say anything back he seemed to have realized that I loved him to and he kissed me. One passionate, love filled kiss.

was gonna stop here but I had nothing else to do...lol GO BOREDOM! I really have no life

The weekend went by quickly, Logan and I just got to know each other. We would just lay on my bed and talk or go to the meadow where he took me to show me his werewolf form. He would talk about his family and what it meant to be a werewolf. It was fascinating what he had to do just as the alpha's son. It was too much for me to keep up with.

I told him about my mother, how she died of cancer, and how my father couldn't look at me, without seeing her. We were in the meadow laying on our backs looking at each other. I loved the way the sunlight fell on my face, warming me. "I don't know. Sometimes I just feel abandoned, but I get it. You know?" I said.

"No, oddly enough, even though I want to kill him for leaving you alone, I get it. I don't know what I'd do if you died. I don't even think I'd live."

I looked at him and gasped. I honestly felt sick at the thought him dead. God now I feel like that stupid Bella in Twilight. I hated her. "Okay, how about this, either of us can die. Okay? We have to die at the same time. Promise me." I said looking into his blue eyes, holding my pinky out to him.

He linked his pinky to mine and said "Deal." Then he held my hand and we sat there in silence, but it was a comfortable silence. We didn't need to talk. "You know, Hayley, I have no idea how I'm going to just go back and be your teacher tomorrow." He said randomly.

But I understood what he was saying. It was going to kill me to watch all those girls flirt with him and not be able to do anything about it. "Well, you are just going to have to."

He sighed and then smirked. "You still have detention." He said with a laugh.

I looked at him with horror! "NO! Mr. Night! Seriously?" I said, realizing too late I hadn't called him by his name.

I looked at him in fear and he grinned wickedly. "What did you just call me?" he said his eyes glinting with evil.

"Logan. I called you Logan." I said in a rush.

"Hayyyy-leyyyy." He sang, but he sounded like the devil. "Punish-ment." Then he rolled on top of me and started to tickle me. I was laughing, and crying at the same time as he kept touching my stomach with his long fingers.

"Please stop. Please stop." I said laughing and giggling, clutching my stomach in pain.

"Nope, this is your punishment."

Now my stomach was in fire. It was in so much pain I was crying from laughing so hard. So there wasn't much I could do. But one thing came to mind. I had to try. If I could keep a straight face long enough. I took my hand and brushed it against his face. "Logan," I cooed, trying not to laugh anymore, even though he was still tickling me. "Please stop." I said seductively. When he paused for a minute I pushed him back and leaned against his chest sitting up right. Kissing his jaw and collar bone lovingly. I could still feel his hands at my stomach.

He was still shocked at my actions when he said, "You shouldn't tease the wolf, Hayley." He said warning me.

Then he looked me once in the eye. I saw lust and want. Then his mouth attacked mine. I gasped in shock. But once he licked my lips I gave into the kiss and wrapped my arms around his neck and moaned. Our tongues were wrestling for dominance, but he ended up winning. "Hayley, please?" he asked, pulling away for a moment then kissing my neck, and pulling my shirt of my head so I was just in my bra and shorts.

"Please what?" I asked breathlessly.

"Can I mate with you?" he asked.

Mate? What? "Huh?" I said pulling away from him quickly. "What does that mean?" I asked.

But before he could answer my phone went off. It was a text from my uncle David. He was home. But the shocking part of the text was Jace was there with him waiting for me. I looked at Logan and said "I have to go. We'll talk about this later. Bye." I said and started to run home. I heard him call from behind me "I'll see you tonight." What did that mean? I shook of all thoughts of that, I'll find out soon enough.

Chapter 12: Mr. Night Get the Hell Outta My House!

Vote and comment people please???? i seriously need some more votes out of selfishness...

I ran home as fast as I could knowing if I didn't get home soon I'd get chewed out and it is seriously something I didn't want to deal with.

I got home sweat dripping down my face my hair messed up into clumps of black. I swore under my breath knowing how awful I looked. I walked through the back door and walked into the living room. "Hey!"

My uncle was sitting on the couch with Jace next to them they were talking about something but when my uncle saw me his face turned bright red with anger. Jace blushed and his eyes looked at me with lust and want. "Hayley Lake! Why the hell don't you have a shirt on?" my uncle screamed at me.

I looked at him in confusion for a minute. I had a shirt on. What was he talking about? I had put one on this morning, a pink tank top with black flowers on it. Then I looked down and realized what he had been talking about. I was in my black shorts with my black bra, I really didn't have a shirt on. "What? How? Huh?" I said not understanding why I didn't have clothes on.

"Hayley-" my uncle started.

"What? I really don't know why I don't have a-" But then it hit me like a semi-truck. Logan had taken off my shirt and I ran here before I could have remembered to put it back on. My face was beat red from embarrassment, so I ran upstairs and to grab a shirt. I got to my room and opened my door and saw a familiar pink tank top. I went to the bed and grabbed it and a note feel from the bed it said.

'Hayley, you left your shirt in clearing. See you tonight. -Logan.'

So he knew I left it. Next time I see him I was going to kill him. I would tear out his eye balls and cut off his- "Hayley, honey, I want to talk to you." My uncle said from outside my door. I put my shirt back on and opened the door. "Yea?" I asked looking at me uncle worried. He was a tall man 6'3 he was well built he made me feel like an ant, just like Logan did. His brown hair and thoughtful eyes reminded me so much of my dad.

He looked at me and said "Well that boy down there got a good show right?"

I blushed a bright red shade of red, I could have sworn I heard a small growl behind me. I turned around and saw no one. "Anyway, that boy, Jace, is he your boyfriend?" he asked.

"What? No!" I said in a shocked voice. Jace? My boyfriend? That was crazy! I started to laugh at the thought of it. "Jace seriously? No. We're just good friends don't worry about it." I said laughing.

"Okay, I just wanted to talk to you. Can we sit down?" he asked pointing to my bed. I nodded and he sat down and patted the space beside him. I plopped down next to me and he cleared his throat.

"Well you know, since your dad has been gone I think I should take the time to talk to you."

"Okay, about what?" I asked nonchalantly.

"Well you know at this age, boys you know will have urges." Oh-my-god....he wasn't. "They will say they like you and then they will only want one thing." He said blushing red, but I swear this was worse on me.

"You aren't seriously having this talk with me?" I asked horrified.

"Well Hayley you are getting older. You should know that sometimes-"

"Okay, David I really don't want to talk about this now okay?"

"Hayley I really don't want to talk about this either but you need to know."

"I know okay? I'm a junior in PUBLIC high school I know about sex. I know about condoms and birth control and stuff like that."

"Hayley I seriously think we should talk about this. One day you are going to find someone you love very much and he is going to want to...do other things with you-"

Okay as awkward as this conversation was all I could think about was Logan and doing things....with him. God I'm a pervert. "David, I'm a virgin. Please let's stop talking about this. I don't have a boyfriend," Okay that was a lie, but seriously how would my uncle take it if he found out I was dating my bio teacher? "And I really don't want to talk about this."

He just looked and me and sighed. "Okay, well then that's that."

I nodded and said "Come on, Jace is still waiting down there, he's probably going to think someone killed us." I said getting up. My uncle looked at me one last time and walked ahead of me out of my room. I could have sworn just before I closed my door I heard laughter.

I shook my head and mumbled to myself "Wow, Hayley you are losing it." When we got back into the room Jace was sitting in the same seat he had been before looking bored and awkward. "Hey." I said and smiled at him.

"Hey," he said getting up and walked towards me "I just came by to see if you were okay after Friday." He said with a sheepish smile.

That was so sweet. "Thanks, no that's great. I'm fine you know? It's fine."

"Oh great that's good." He said awkwardly, "Well okay I guess I'll just leave, now that I know your find."

I laughed and said "Yea thanks for stopping by, that's really nice of you."

"Yea. Well..." he said heading towards the door.

"Hey, Jace?" I asked when he was half way to his car. He turned and looked at me "You want to sit with me at lunch tomorrow?" I asked, I don't know why but for some reason I didn't want to be away from him. What the hell was going on?

He just smirked and said "Yea, that'd be nice. See you tomorrow." And he got in his car and drove away.

I sighed and walked back into the house feeling sad. My uncle was on the phone and he looked worried. "Jim I don't think I can, I know it's important but I just got home." He stopped talking for awhile listening to the other end "It's really that bad?" he asked nervous "Fine I'll come in." he slammed the phone down and sighed looking tired. He saw me watching him and said "Hayley honey I got to go back to the station."

I looked at him, he looked as if he was going to drop dead. "You sure you're up for it? You looked exhausted." I said worried.

"Yea, I'll be home around 9 okay?"

I nodded and just like that I was alone and the house was empty. I walked around for a bit thinking of some way to do. It was only five o'clock and I really didn't want to go to bed. I was pretty sure I had all my homework done. I sat down on the couch and turned the tv on. I just flipped aimlessly through the channels finding nothing to watch. I just turned off the tv when I gave up. I grabbed a book from the coffee table and started reading. But I soon gave up, it was To Kill a Mockingbird by Harper Lee, I've read the book hundreds of times so I soon got bored.

I got back up at looked at the clock. It was five thirty and I still had nothing to do. I sighed in annoyance and went to the kitchen and started to make dinner. I grabbed the things I needed and suddenly felt a pair of arms go around my waist. I screamed bloody murder and whipped around looking for something to hit the perpetrator with. I saw a knife of the counter and lunged to grab it. But the arms held me back. "Please let go of me." I screamed.

I was still just screaming when I heard a familiar laughter. "Hayley, chill it's just me." I turned around and saw Logan looking at me with amusement in his eyes.

"What? How did you get in here?" I asked shocked.

"It's really easy to get into your house." He said not really answering my question.

I just sighed and said "Move it, I've got to make dinner."

Logan just laughed and let me go. I chopped up dices of chicken while the rice was in the microwave. Then I fried up eggs and cup up vegetables. Once everything was ready I threw it all in a huge pan and added soy sauce. I felt awkward and uncomfortable knowing he was watching me. "Go away." I said.

He just laughed and said "Do you really want me to go away?"

"Yes." I said unsure.

"Too bad!"

"Don't you have anything else to do?" I asked annoyed.

"Nope, plus where you are is where I want to be." He said looking at me with intense eyes.

I blushed red and said "That was cliché."

He smiled and said "Yes but it's true."

I sighed and finished dinner I made three plates, I handed Logan one wrapped one up and put it in the fridge and then I ate one for myself. Logan and I sat at the kitchen table and just talked about nothing and everything important. We laughed about weird things and had weird conversations. Being with him felt so right it freaked me out. He cleaned the dished while I got to sit back and make fun of him.

When it was time for bed I pushed him out the door, literally and then ran up to bed. I took a quick shower and went back into my room with a towel wrapped around my body. I went to my closet and took out shorts and a t-shirt and I turned to set them on my bed when I saw Logan sitting there staring at me. "Oh my god!" I screeched. "When the hell did you get in here?"

He laughed and said "Awhile, nice body."

I covered up as much as I could and ran back into the bathroom and got changed. I went back out to my room and saw he was lying on my bed. I was too tired to be mad so I lay next to him and cuddled up to him. "I'm mad at you." I said as he wrapped his arms around me."

"Why?" he said while dragging his hands through my wet hair.

"You knew I didn't have a top on when I ran home, you also show up randomly which is annoying."

"Well about the top I'm not too happy since that stupid Jace got to see you without it. And I need you by my side I hate when you aren't there." He said. I sighed happily and fell asleep.

David's POV:

I go to the station and hunted down Jim. When I saw him I went up to him and asked "So let's see the damage."

He looked at me with a haggard face, "It's bad David." He said leading me to the coroner's office. We stepped inside and I looked at the body that was laying on the slab of metal.

"Hey David." Said Joe, the medical examiner. "He had a broken neck, no facial wounds. It's rather odd because besides the broken neck John Doe looks perfect."

"Okay, well why am I here?" I asked annoyed.

"Well David he was drained of all his blood." Oh shit.

Hayley's POV:

When I woke up I reached for the space next to me, it was empty. I sat up and looked for Logan he wasn't there. But there was a note.

"Dear Hayley,

I woke up around 5, I had to get home and change. See you in school. By the way did you do your bio homework? Cya in class.

-Love Logan.

Ps. remember you have detention too and if you skip i'm going to punish you."

Bio homework? Oh crap! I forgot! This week has been so crazy I forgot my bio homework. Logan Night I am going to kill you. I got changed and ran outside and walked to school, swearing under my breath. I got to school on time and met an angry Jane and Noah at my locker.

"Okay Hayley Lake you have some major explaining to do." Jane started off.

"We haven't heard a word from you all weekend. Do you know how worried we were?" Noah shouted at me.

"Sorry guys, it's just been a weird week." I said feeling guilty I couldn't tell them what was really happening.

"No matter how weird it was you could have called your best friends."

"I'm sorry." I said hanging my head.

They both let out a sigh and said at the same time. "It's okay we forgive you. But you're paying for lunch."

I let out a laugh in relief and said "Deal." Then I turned around to quickly and ran into a solid figure. "Ouch!" I said falling to the ground and spilling my books all over the floor. I looked up and saw a boy I have never seen before. He was around 6'3, brown hair and brown eyes. He was as pale as snow, his had spider bits below his lips and earrings in his ears. He looked at me and frowned, his blood red lips turning down into a grimace. "Sorry," I said meekly.

He bent down slowly not saying a word and picked up my books and helped me up. "Thanks." I said smiling at me. He looked at me funny for a minute and smiled a breath taking smile back at me. "So are you new here?" I asked.

"Yea," he said quietly.

"I'm Hayley I'm a junior. How about you?"

"I'm Andrew, I'm a senior this year."

"Oh that's cool. Where are you from?"

He opened his mouth to answer me but then the bell rang. "Hey Andrew, I got to go! But we'll talk later okay?"

He nodded and walked away. I watched as his hulky figure walked down the hallway, people seemed to part like the red sea when he walked by. I sighed and ran to class.

All too soon it was time to go into Logan's, Mr. Night's class and I was nervous and annoyed at the same time. He was my boyfriend but when the girls in class would start to flirt with him I would not be able to say a thing. I walked into class looking at the floor and went and sat in the back table in the corner away from everyone. I could feel someone's gaze but I just looked down at the table refusing to look up. Noah and Jane soon sat next to me talking about something I really didn't care about. Then the class started.

"So everyone I'm going to come by and collect your homework. Have it ready by the time I get to your desk." Logan said with amusement in his voice.

I sighed in annoyance, I hadn't done it, and he probably knew I didn't. He stopped at our desk and Noah and Jane handed him their homework. I looked up at him with a look that said 'I hate you and want your head on a stick.' "Miss. Lake, where is your homework." He said trying not to smile.

"I didn't do it."

"Why didn't you?"

"I didn't have time." I said annoyed.

"Why not?" he asked.

I glared at him, he knew why the hell not and he was doing this to tick me off. "I was busy trying to kill a certain someone."

"Oh and who might that be?" he asked completely amused.

"None of your business." I snapped.

He laughed and said "After class Miss. Lake." I groaned, I really wanted to kill him. He walked away and collected everyone's papers.

"She is just doing this to get close to him. She is such a slut." Blake said to Amy.

"Yea she is." Amy agreed. I just ignored the comment. Logan started to talk about something I couldn't follow so I slowly drifted off to sleep.

I was woken up by the bell, my head shot up and Jane and Noah were laughing at me. "Hey we'll meet you at lunch seeing as you have to stay after with that hunk of a teacher." Jane said with a wink and left.

I slowly walked up to Logan's desk once the room was clear. I then processed to hit him across the head. "What was that for?" he asked.

"For giving me shit in class." I said annoyed.

"Oh that? That was fun."

"Go die." I said and started to walk out.

"Hey Hayley what are you doing?"

"Leaving."

"Why?"

"I'm mad at you."

"I'm your teacher you have to do what I say." He said cockily.

"Screw you!" I shouted and ran out the door and running into for the second time today Andrew. "Oh Andrew!" I said happily. "Why are you here?" I asked, this was the junior wing why would a senior be here?

"I need to talk to a Mr. Night, is this his room?"

"Yea." I said cautiously. He walked around me and into the room with me at this heels. "Logan Night" Andrew said.

Logan looked up from his desk his eyes getting wider in shock. "Andrew McVergan, what the hell are you doing here?" he asked, his voice ringing with disbelief.

"My coven is here because of a recent disturbance."

Coven? "Hayley, leave." Logan said.

"Logan what does he mean?" I asked stepping around Andrew and stood by Logan's side. "Hayley just leave."

"Why?" I asked annoyed.

"Because he's a vampire."

blah blah blah blah comment and vote!

Chapter 13: Mr. Heart Breaker is back

Hayley's pov:

Vampire? Andrew was a vampire? Vampires were real? Why wouldn't they be real? Werewolves are real shouldn't vampires be real as well? But for some unknown reason I have never thought of that. "Like twilight?" I asked confused.

I could feel Logan's annoyance but Andrew was laughing."Well not like Twilight. We DO have fangs we ALL have powers, I'm not afraid of the sun, it doesn't bother any of us. And as far as I know I like human blood. Animal is fine I guess but we couldn't live solely on that. We'd die."

"Oh." I said. I heard Logan sighed. I looked at him questionably.

"You aren't afraid of vampires? You aren't afraid of werewolves? You have got to be the weirdest person I have ever met."

"I take great offense to that. And I'm already mad at you. But no I'm not afraid of either of you because you honestly don't seem scary." the moment that came out of my mouth I knew I would regret it.

Logan's and Andrew's features sharpened and they both looked at me with a terrifying look, as if daring me to say more. I just shrunk back "I am afraid of fish though." I said quickly hoping to distract them.

And it worked. Logan and Andrew were cracking up laughing looking at me funny. "You are a very strange girl." Andrew said laughing.

Logan who was unable to talk due to the fact he was laughing so hard. This made me furious. I hated it when he made fun of me. Once he finally caught his breathe he said "Hayley, I worry about you sometimes. Are you okay in the head?"

"Logan stop! Seriously! I hate it when you make fun of me." I said.

"Sorry, you are just too fun to bully. Now anyways Andrew why would you leeches need any help from us?" Logan said with distain in his voice. He obviously didn't like Andrew, or vampires I guess.

"Well dog, we have a truce right? This involves your kind too. There is something out there. Something we've never came across before. We have found several vampires dead in the last few weeks, and these aren't fledglings either. These are vampires that have been around for centuries. Also there have been dozens of humans killed, drained of blood. And don't go thinking we did it. I make sure my covens feed outside of this area." Andrew said looking at Logan with worried eyes.

I looked at Logan who was in deep thought. "Okay I see. Hayley, leave now okay?"

"What why?" I complained.

"Because this isn't any of your business." He said his voice ice cold.

"Logan what involves you is my business."

"Hayley I'm not asking you again, leave now." He looked at me, his eyes cold and void of any emotion.

"Okay fine then." I said and stormed out the door. It was lunch and I was so pissed I didn't even feel like eating. But I had told Jane and Noah I'd pay of their lunch. So I huffed my way down to the cafeteria, still angry. Jane and Noah were sitting down waiting for me. When they saw my face they looked at each other with worried looks. "Are you okay?" they asked.

I couldn't really tell them that my werewolf teacher of a boyfriend was being a prissy girl and decided not to tell me anything. So I just shook my head and threw ten dollars on the table. "Here, get your lunch." They were great friends, they seemed to understand that I didn't want to talk about it. So they left and got their food. I sat down at the table and put my Ipod head buds in my head and played the first song that came up. It was Bittersweet Symphony by the Verve. I set my head on the desk and tired not to cry. I don't know how I became like this. I was so emotional all the time. I felt pathetic. So I just sat there trying not to think. "HEY HAYLEY!" a voice said pulling me out of my day dreams.

I looked up it was Jace. I smiled at him and said, "Hey what's up?"

"Nothing, offer still stands right?"

"What?" I asked confused.

"You said I could sit here yesterday, does the offer still stand?" he said and smiled sweetly at me.

"Oh yea, sorry yea! I'd like that."

He smiled at me again and said "Are you okay? You look, sad?"

"Yea, I'm fine just really tired you know?"

"Yea I get it." he said awkwardly. "Oh yea! I've been meaning to ask you something."

"Yea."

"You want to go to a movie after school today? I just thought it might be fun. You know a little cheer up?"

I looked at him confused. Why would he want to hang out with me? Did I really care? I was just about to say yes until I thought of Logan. No matter how mad I was at him being with Jace made me feel like I was cheating on Logan and I never wanted to do that. I loved Logan and I never wanted to do something that made him mad at me. "I would, it sounds like fun but I can't. I have detention after school with Mr. Night."

"Oh, maybe some other time."

"Yea that would be fun." The rest of lunch was awkward but Noah and Jane helped out a little by trying to make things fun. Both of them would talk about the weirdest things making all of us laugh.

The day went by quickly and Logan was the only thing I could think of. I made my way to his room after school, before I opened the door I looked up through the window. I saw Logan was in there, but not alone. He was with Jasmine and they were kissing. Tears flowed to my eyes and poured out uncontrollably. I just watched as they continued to kiss, he wasn't pulling away. How could he do this? My chest felt as though it was being ripped open, a violent shutter filled my body as I cried out in pain. I ducked when I saw them both turn. I heard footsteps come towards the door. I looked up afraid to see Logan's face knowing it would crush me. But it wasn't Logan I saw, it was Jasmine. She saw me and smirked and then called back "It's no one. I'm glad your mother convinced you to mate with me other than that stupid high school girl. I'm also glad you agreed the moment she asked." Then she laughed and walked back into the room.

I got up and ran through the hallways and out the door, with tears streaming down my face. And of course it was raining, why did this always happen? Could my life get any worse? But I guess it couldn't.

I saw Jace standing leaning on his car looking at me with worry on his

face. He ran up to me and hugged me. I fought his warm embrace at

first but when I couldn't fight anymore I hugged him back and cried.

9 781805 107118